FOX HUNT

ALSO IN THE RED RAIN SERIES

Red Rain
Project 74
Crook Q
Prisoner 120518
Andromeda
Aurelius
Fox Hunt
Catalyst

FOX HUNT

RED RAIN #4

RACHEL NEWHOUSE

ISBN-13: 978-1-957432-10-6

Cover Art by Clarissa Laurenda (Instagram: @fungzauu_)
Cover Layout by Shawn Jonas

This is a work of fiction. Any similarities to real people, living or dead, are merely coincidental.

All Scripture quotations, unless otherwise indicated, are taken from the Holy Bible, New International Version®, NIV®. Copyright ©1973, 1978, 1984, 2011 by Biblica, Inc.™ Used by permission of Zondervan. All rights reserved worldwide. www.zondervan.com The "NIV" and "New International Version" are trademarks registered in the United States Patent and Trademark Office by Biblica, Inc.™

rachelnewhouse.com

To SBP
What would I do without you?

Fail miserably, probably.

JUNE 2076

1

Of all the ways I had imagined spending my Sunday afternoon, getting a tattoo with Nic in the ghetto of a Martian city was nowhere on the list.

Well, "tattoo" was a bit of a misnomer; in reality, it was a minor cosmetic surgery. "Just like getting a nose job," the technician explained as he swiftly slid my fingers into the metal device that would keep them still for the delicate procedure. "Relax, babe."

I was doing no such thing. Lying in a cracked dentist's chair in the shuttered back room of a tattoo parlor with both hands strapped down was giving my anxiety a lot of material to work with. The only thing keeping my heart from forcing its way up my throat was the fact that Nic stood behind me, watching.

I was a bit surprised that he'd come with me, especially when the procedure was supposed to take several hours. But I wasn't about to complain. He stood with arms crossed and feet apart, eyes roaming the room in constant patrol. The bulge of the pistol in his pocket sent a clear message.

The technician finished strapping me in and rolled the surgery machine up to the chair. It was sleek and metallic—a single robotic arm with a microscopic needle on the end. The technician keyed a passcode into the control panel, and the device whirred to life. The robotic arm stretched and rotated, needle sliding in and out.

"Did you sanitize that?" Nic grunted.

The technician mumbled something as he fetched an alcohol pad and swiped it on the needle. I swallowed.

"Now this won't hurt much," the technician said for the tenth time. I noted that his qualifiers kept changing; five minutes ago, the procedure wasn't supposed to hurt "one bit."

"This laser-guided needle is going to alter your fingerprints—like a miniature skin graft. But first, we have to design your new set. And that's why you pay me the big bucks." He rolled his chair up to the control panel and typed eagerly.

"*How* much is this going to be?" I asked.

"It's fine," Nic interrupted, and I silenced.

"First, I scan your existing prints. Then I run them through a program that compares them to a global database so the algorithm can generate a new pattern. Of course, I always manually edit my designs to make sure they look as organic as possible. Purely autogenerated prints look fake—if you ask me."

He threw a pierced-lip grin at me that I didn't return. I had no idea if any of that was true, but I didn't have much of a choice. I had to get new prints taken before I could use my new file, and there weren't that many microsurgeons on Mars.

At least not many who were willing to do procedures off the record.

The technician guided the machine's arm until it hovered above my left hand. A patchwork of blue laser light fell on my thumb. A soft whir and a click, and then he moved on to the next finger.

I tried to control my rising panic as he scanned the rest of my digits. My fingerprints had been with me since birth. God had designed them Himself, and within three hours they would all be irreversibly altered.

After today, Philadelphia Smyrna would no longer exist, and Andromeda Nolan would take her place.

The design process took over an hour, during which I closed my eyes and prayed to keep myself from hyperventilating. There wasn't much else I could do with my hands bolted to the arms of the chair.

Finally, the technician called Nic over to approve the prints. He squinted at them, then angled the screen so I could see.

I stared at the eerie electronic rendering, as if I had any idea what I was looking for. *Dear God, I hope this is the right choice.* I looked up at the technician and nodded.

"One new ID coming up! Let me know if it starts hurting a lot."

The machine shifted gears. The laser changed from a grid to a dot, so focused I could barely see it. Then without any kind of warning, the needle sank into my skin.

I flinched as the thin metal started weaving in and out of my fingertip. My heart broke free and blocked my next breath, everything in me begging him to stop. I couldn't do this—I couldn't take who I had been my entire life and callously throw that person away like I was erasing a whiteboard.

I was Philadelphia Smyrna. I was.

But I couldn't be, not anymore. I knew that. I knew it wasn't safe. My "real" name and image had been plastered all over the internet, associated with several acts of terrorism against the United—some of which I was more or less responsible for. Even worse, I was their link to Red Rain.

If I didn't want to end up in an interrogation room giving the government the formula to melt entire cities with acid rain, I needed to become a new person. So I closed my eyes, bit down on my tongue, and said nothing.

It seemed like an eternity before the microscopic stabbing stopped. It hadn't hurt much—although I'm sure the pain medication Nic doped me up on before we left had an effect. The technician freed my hands from the machine, and I struggled to feel them. My palms tingled and shook, my fingertips flushed red and raw.

"And there you have it, Miss—what did you say your name was?"

I was about to answer when Nic stepped between us. "I'm paying." He held out his phone. The technician took it and keyed in numbers.

"How much extra to wipe the originals?" Nic waved his hand at the machine.

The technician licked his lip piercing. Then he grinned, hit another key, and handed the phone back to Nic.

Nic nodded and pocketed the device. "Let's go."

I tested my balance before standing up, then followed him out the door into the main storefront. The place was deserted except for another tattoo artist, who lay on her table scrolling through a phone.

"Want anything else done while you're here?" The technician came out behind us and waved his hand at the sketches plastered on the wall.

"No thank you," I said, even as my eyes scanned the gallery. Although most of it was downright bizarre, I had to admit that a few of the pieces—like a stunning blue-and-purple nebula wrapped around someone's wrist—were strangely alluring.

He shrugged. "Come back anytime if you change your mind."

Nic was already out the door, so I hurried to follow. "You know, he's not wrong," Nic commented as soon as we had blended into the anonymity of the alley. "A tattoo is a fairly inexpensive way to change your appearance."

"You want to sign the parental waiver on that?"

He grunted at me as he unlocked the transfer. Even though Nic had agreed to be Andromeda's legal guardian on paper, he did not like being reminded.

I grabbed the passenger door handle and winced, my tender fingertips protesting. I swallowed a grimace as I opened the door and hoisted myself over the treads into our bulky ride. Nic slid into the driver's seat.

"Besides," I said as buckled in, "I was hoping for less permanent options."

"If you want to spend an hour in the bathroom putting on your mask each morning, be my guest. Just be glad you don't pay the water bill."

He started the transfer and pulled out of the parking lot. I took one last look at the Martian city as we drove down the backroad towards the border. We were on the outskirts, where the buildings were smaller and cheaper, but it was still a sight to behold.

The architecture was a mishmash of designs, as if no one could decide what aesthetic Mars should adopt. Most of the buildings were paneled with large windows to let in as much of the distant sunlight as possible. Slabs of concrete traced out an informal network of roads, and numerous planter boxes and greenhouses attempted to lend some humanity to the inorganic maze. Here and there, the natural red earth seeped through the cracks in the road and the gaps between buildings, reminding us that we were ultimately foreigners superimposing our will on an unforgiving wilderness.

Above it all stretched a dome of glass. The honeycomb panels kept the thin atmosphere out and the heat in—or at least some of it. Despite the fact that we were near the equator and had been soaking in the sun all day, Nic had still advised me to wear my heaviest jacket. He cranked the heat up in the car as we neared the edge of the glass.

The border officer cleared Nic's credentials, then flagged us into an exit tunnel. We drove into a bay, and the doors behind us shut, plunging us into near-darkness. Nic double- and triple-checked that all the vehicle's windows were sealed and the doors locked. After a moment's hesitation, the lights on the wall flashed green. The doors ahead of us opened, and we drove out into the Martian countryside.

The town was one of three biodomes clustered in the valley. I watched the other cities glitter in the distance as we drove up the crude road that had been hewn into the side of the plateau. We crested the top and continued into the unsettled wilderness. Around us stretched miles of untouched dirt. There were no roads, no signs, no other indication that humans lived on this planet. The transfer's computer navigated off of some unseen satellite as it led us through the gathering darkness.

I risked conversation. "Thanks for your help back there."

"Oh, you're paying me back."

I turned to him. "That's not what I meant."

He didn't respond or look at me, so I kept silent and returned my attention to the shadowy outcrops rolling past.

It was dark by the time we got back to Base #9.6.11. It was the only research base for miles in this part of the country, and the light from the glass-domed central wing shone like a lighthouse in the wilderness. I swore the base looked bigger every time I saw it from the outside. New wings and biodomes were always being added, connected by snaking hallways, as if the base were a living organism sending out roots and multiplying.

The docking bay doors opened to receive us. We waited until they had closed again and the atmosphere had been restored before piling out of the car.

Nic opened the door to the base, took two steps into the lobby, and stopped.

"You know I'm not doing this just for you, right?" he said without turning around.

"Huh?"

"I'm not giving you all this tender loving care because I like you."

"Good, because I thought we were past the stage of having to like each other."

He glanced back at me. "If you screw this up, I go down with you."

That wasn't exactly what he said, but it was the child-friendly translation.

"If the United ever figures out who 'Andromeda' really is, they're going to investigate her relatives—and at the moment, that is, unfortunately, me."

"Is that why you didn't want me to pay?"

He nodded. "I don't want you logging any electronic activity off this base until your new file is online." He started walking. "Find Jean-Luc and have him scan your prints into the database. Have him text me when he's done. The sooner we get your new file online, the better."

2

It took me awhile to find Jean-Luc, if only because I had no idea who he was. Thankfully, my neighbor Mr. Sardis was, as always, happy to help me, and within an hour my new prints were imaged and uploaded.

I went back to the cafeteria to claim the tail end of dinner, then retired to my quarters. I braced myself as I waved my hand over the panel and opened the door. I hated seeing the empty room and being reminded that I lived alone.

I went to the bathroom and started stripping my "mask," as Nic called it. A whole process had gone into getting me ready to go to town. Temporary dye turned my long, dark hair an unnatural shade of maroon, and contacts had shifted my brown eyes green. A heavy layer of makeup contoured my face, and I'd cobbled together an ill-fitting outfit from pieces Mrs. Sardis had lent me. The whole process had taken over an hour, and taking it apart took at least half that—all so that nobody on the street would recognize me as Blue Fire, the girl from the videos.

Nic was right—I was glad I didn't pay the water bill.

Three shampoos later, my hair had been restored to its natural color, conditioned, and braided to dry. I wandered back to the living room to hear my tablet dinging.

I picked it up. I still wasn't sure that I liked the new device. It was as thin as a clipboard, with sharp edges and a too-bright screen. I missed the comforting warmth of my clunky old ereader, with its bulky case and clacking buttons. This tablet didn't even have a home button; it turned on as soon as it saw my face.

I sank down on the couch and swiped through the notifications. There weren't many, mostly because so few people knew how to contact me. Unfortunately, I had to keep it that way.

I did have a couple of new texts on my encrypted messaging app. The most recent was from Nic.

IT'S UP

I swallowed, feeling the significance of that settle in my stomach. As far as the government was concerned, I was now Andromeda Nolan.

I whispered the name to myself, still trying to get used to the sound. I didn't love the name, mainly because I didn't love the man who had given it to me. Director Thames Nolan had picked it when he'd forged the file. He had been intending to adopt me—after he used me to blackmail my father into completing the formula for Red Rain. It would have worked if I hadn't exposed Thames's secrets on livestream and turned him over to the United.

He'd taken the easy way out, and I had no choice but to assume the identity he'd designed for me. I hated using his last name; every time I said it, I thought of him and his sickeningly sweet wife. But Philadelphia's file was a mess, and I had to start over if I had any hope of surviving.

Nic sent another message.

WILL FIX YOUR TABLET TOMORROW AT
BREAKFAST

I texted back a "k, thanks" and shoved the thoughts out of
my head. I switched over to the other unread conversation: from
Jayde—or "Aurelius," as he went by online.

HEY, YOU OKAY? HAVEN'T SEEN YOU ONLINE
ALL DAY

I pondered the message before replying. I wanted to spill my
whole day to him; telling a sympathetic ear how I had just wiped
my fingerprints and become a new person would probably make
me feel better about the ordeal. But Nic had been very, extremely,
and somewhat violently strict about making sure I didn't
mention Andromeda online. As long as the United still thought I
was going by Philadelphia, they would be watching the wrong
file.

So even though I trusted Jayde—the kindly guard had
helped me out of more than one scrape—I'd obeyed Nic and not
told Jayde I had new credentials.

After writing and rewriting my reply several times in my
head, I settled for:

ALL GOOD, JUST TAKING CARE OF A FEW THINGS.
ANY WORD?

I knew what the answer would be—if there had been any
word, he would have blown my texts up—but the irrational
amount of hope that gripped my life demanded I ask.

NONE. I'M SORRY, PHIL

I sighed. The breath grated against my buried emotion, and
a half-formed sob ripped out of me. I closed my eyes and curled
into the couch, trying to shut out the sight of the empty room,
the heavy silence, and the crushing reminder that I had no idea
where my family was.

It had been two weeks since Thames died, and there was still no activity on either my father's or brother's files. Nic's sister Cea had also gone dark. Last I knew they were on Earth; they'd escaped from Thames and gone off the grid. I thought, now that Thames was gone, they would realize I was safe and try to make contact—if not with me, then at least with our mutual friends in the underground.

But so far there had been radio silence.

Jayde tried to console me.

8 MILLION PEOPLE SAW YOUR LAST VIDEO THOUGH. EVERYONE'S TALKING ABOUT BLUE FIRE

I tried to muster the energy to be impressed by that. It didn't matter if a *billion* people saw my video if that number didn't include the three people I was searching for.

AND NO ONE'S SAID *ANYTHING*? NOTHING IN THE COMMENTS?

NOTHING YET. MY NETWORK IS ON HIGH ALERT—IF THEY MAKE CONTACT WITH ANYONE, WE'LL BE THE FIRST TO KNOW

I drummed my nails on the screen. It didn't make sense. Why *hadn't* they made contact with the underground? I knew Dad and Ephesus had to be careful; their files were as corrupted as Philadelphia's. But Cea had never been incriminated in the investigation into Red Rain. Her file was clean. She knew how to find Jayde. She could easily make contact—or even turn herself in at our old religious containment camp. So why hadn't she?

I banged my frustration out on the keyboard.

ANY OTHER IDEAS?

The typing dots appeared at the bottom of the screen, vanished, then reappeared several moments later.

YOU COULD TRY TELLING THEM TO ORDER PIZZA

I stiffened. "Order pizza" was their euphemism for calling for an emergency pickup. Cea and I had done it once, but that was before Stanyard, the former friend who used to "deliver" that pizza, had abandoned me in an alley to die.

Was he back in the game? I resisted the urge to ask; I knew Jayde couldn't tell me in so many words. Did it even matter? Stanyard had been quick to betray me before, and now the stakes were much higher. He was the last person I trusted with my family's safety.

I DON'T TRUST HIM

Jayde's response was quick.

SOMEONE ELSE RUNS THE SHOP NOW

CAN I TRUST THEM?

OF COURSE

I searched for a sense of peace about the whole thing and only found residual pain and bitterness.

I DON'T KNOW. I'D RATHER THEY CALL YOU

YEAH, BUT YOU CAN'T GIVE OUT MY PHONE NUMBER ON AIR

I sighed. *Nor mine.*

JUST TELL THEM TO ORDER PIZZA. THEY KNOW WHERE THE SHOP IS

He was right, and it was better than nothing. There was only so much I could do from Mars.

OKAY

I PROMISE WE'LL FIGURE THIS OUT, PHIL. WE'LL
FIND THEM. YOU CAN TRUST ME

I tried to absorb his confidence. *Please, God. I need you.*

I thanked Jayde, said goodbye, pulled up Sydney's number. Sydney was a tech on base that I wouldn't know from Adam, except that he could run the soundboard in the recording studio. I preferred him over the other techs—mainly because he didn't talk much and had a tendency to be up late.

UP FOR A RUN?

After a few minutes, he responded.

SURE. LET ME FINISH THIS GAME

I thanked him and left my dorm to start the long trek back to Wing 74.

It had taken several tries—most of which ended with me calling Mr. Sardis to come rescue me—before I could walk there without getting lost. My route was definitely not the most efficient, but it was the one I could remember, so I stuck with it.

Nic had already started remodeling Wing 74. A good chunk of it had been demolished; the rest was being retrofitted and reconfigured. Hallways were rerouted, rooms were stripped and repurposed, and windows were added to wings that had formerly been denied the light of day. All with the intent of covering up what had really happened in these halls.

Nic said it was so that should Carnegie, his former assistant, ever rat us out and send officials to investigate the base, they wouldn't find anything linking the base to Red Rain or Thames. Me, I was just glad I was no longer locked on the wrong side of the door.

All of the doors in Wing 74 opened for me now. Nic had given me all access.

At my request, there was one room in Wing 74 that would survive the demo—the recording studio. Although I had no fond memories of that room either, it was currently my best hope for finding my family.

I pushed aside the drop cloth that shielded the door from construction dust and let myself in. While I waited, I straightened the greenscreen, centered the chair, and polished the lens of the gigantic robotic camera that hung from the ceiling.

Sydney arrived about the time I was satisfied with my work. He appeared in the plexiglass window of the sound booth and started flicking on monitors. "Tell me when you're ready to start," he said, which was probably the only thing he'd say to me all evening.

I nodded and arranged myself in the chair. The viewscreen of the camera flickered on, and I checked myself in the monitor. I hadn't bothered to put on makeup, so I looked ashen and tired in the stark glare of the studio lighting. I didn't care. Ironically, on camera was the one place I could be myself without a filter.

There was no reason to hide online; the world already knew who Philadelphia Smyrna was. Thames and Carnegie had forced me to record videos for their various and sundry evil schemes, and my name—and the hashtag #bluefire, which they'd evidently invented to channel the energy—had been trending for a few weeks now.

I was trying to use my forced popularity to my own advantage. Thames had been using my videos to try and find my father; surely I could do the same. Jayde and his friends were sharing my content religiously, and the internet loved my tragic life story. As long as I included some clickbait content about the ugly truth of the United—and what they did to unassimilated people like me—my videos blew up. Eventually my family had to see one of them.

Of course, I couldn't exactly leave a forwarding address or tell them to meet me at the corner of 18th and Vine, not when United officials would love to arrest and/or execute all of us. Maintaining a stable online presence had also proved impossible;

the government banned all my accounts as soon as they found them.

But I wasn't about to give up. My family was out there somewhere; until the Holy Spirit told me otherwise, I would keep praying and sending up smoke signals.

I gave Sydney the go-ahead, took a deep breath, and stared straight into the camera. The *On Air* sign on the wall glowed to life.

"My name is Philadelphia Smyrna, and I'm looking for my father."

3

Nic met me for breakfast the next morning. He approached my table with a coffee cup in one hand and the other outstretched. I dutifully pulled my tablet out of my pouch and handed it to him.

He sat across from me, drained the last of his mug, and started toggling menus.

"Do you need more coffee?" I asked in lieu of the good morning he had noticeably omitted.

"This shouldn't be *that* hard," he said without looking up. "But if you're offering."

I got up and took his mug to the buffet to get him a refill. I had seen him drink enough of the stuff that I knew how he liked it—as black as it came.

I returned to the table and set the mug down in front of him, using the opportunity to watch over his shoulder as long as I could before he got annoyed.

"What are you doing to it?" I asked, trying to sound innocently curious. I'd gotten used to him messing with my stuff—it was his tablet, after all—but I still liked to know what he was changing.

"I'm officially registering this device on the United's database."

I was so appalled by that statement that I froze.

"Don't hover over my shoulder. We talked about this, Andi."

"You can call me Phil," I reminded him for at least the seventh time that week, "and why?"

"Because I can't work when you're reading over my shoulder. Now sit down."

"Not that," I groused, but did it anyway. "Why are you registering my tablet with the United?"

"For the same reason I call you Andromeda—so you can be legally compliant."

I tried to rationalize that on my own and failed. "Since when have you cared about making sure stuff is legal?"

He spared me a sharp glance over the edge of the tablet. "Ninety percent of my job is making sure this place stays legal. Believe me, if I didn't have to make sure we check all the boxes, I'd get a *lot* more done."

"So what box did you check when Ephesus 'died'?"

"'Deceased.'"

"Hilarious."

He shrugged. "That's what the United needed to hear. As governor, I'm responsible for everything that happens on base. That means I need to be able to reconcile everything—and everyone—that comes or goes. In the case of your brother, I needed to explain why I didn't have a living person *or* a body. Transit explosion was the most reasonable explanation at the time."

The tablet chirped at him. "Although in hindsight, I probably could have found a less dramatic solution."

It was my turn to shrug. "So you're saying there's a paper trail for everything that happens on base, even if the details are a bit embellished?"

"Mmhmm," he mumbled around a sip of coffee.

"How does registering my tablet help? Wouldn't it be easier to leave it in incognito mode or whatever and not tell them the device exists?"

"While you're on base, sure, because I'm the only one watching the internet traffic. But as soon as you connect to someone else's wifi, having an unregistered device will raise huge red flags. It's like walking into a bank with a mask on—they're going to assume you're up to no good."

He looked up and met my eyes. "What I'm about to tell you is very important. I need you to listen carefully, because I am *not* going back to jail because you did something stupid on TikTok."

I leaned back and returned his gaze. "I still don't know what that is, but okay."

"This device is now officially registered as belonging to Andromeda Nolan." He held the tablet up for emphasis. "Which means, don't do *anything* on it that Andromeda wouldn't do."

"Got it."

"That means you're not Philadelphia, and Dr. Smyrna isn't your dad."

I flinched.

Nic was unmerciful. "I mean it, Andromeda. If you mention any names online—make any association with yourself and the Smyrnas—someone could make the connection, and then your whole online presence is ruined. Andromeda is only safe as long as you protect her."

"I know," I whispered, still shivering.

"Which means..." He laid my tablet on the table and resumed typing. "That boyfriend of yours needs to stop calling you 'Phil.'"

"Jayde?" I questioned, then blushed. "He's not my boyfriend. Stop making it weird."

"*He's* the one making it weird. He's been acting awful chummy for someone who is, at best, a lead." He flicked his finger across the screen, and I knew without asking that he was skimming my chat history. "He should know his chats could be watched."

My skin crawled, partially from fear and partially because I wasn't sure how I felt about Nic reading my conversations with Jayde. We hadn't talked about anything but finding my family, but I still didn't want Nic as a third wheel. "I thought you said that app was secure. Well, semi-secure."

"It's semi-secure because it disguises itself. It cloaks the data to make it look like you're playing a multiplayer game online instead of texting. That's how it hides the data exchange between two users. Most algorithms will glaze right over it—but if a censor does decide to investigate, the code isn't hard to crack."

He typed with both hands. "I'm going to wipe your chat history and create a new account for you. Don't worry—I'll let him know you'll be in touch when you need him."

I could tell by the amount of characters he was producing that he was also telling Jayde much more than that—no doubt reading him the riot act about revealing my identity online. I cringed and reached for the tablet. "Let me do it."

"Already done." He punched a button.

I hissed at him.

He arched an eyebrow.

I too was a little mortified by the sound that had come out of my mouth, but I was no less upset. "You could have let me talk to him."

"Sorry, but this was important."

That made it ten times worse. "Oh, so you don't trust me with important stuff?"

His eyebrow seemed stuck up there. "Don't be a child."

"Don't be a jerk," I shot back, and slumped in the chair. The deed was done, so it was pointless to argue, but the anger still sizzled in my nerves. Jayde was my friend, the one relationship I had outside of this base, and I didn't like Nic speaking on my behalf. If Jayde needed to be put in his place, I wanted to be the one to tell him; it was my relationship to manage.

Apparently Nic thought we were even on exchanging insults, because he let it drop. He clicked another button and handed the tablet back to me.

I looked at the screen. The messaging app was loaded under a brand-new account with no chat history. I couldn't even read what he'd told Jayde.

Nic returned to his coffee. "Now that you're online, you can pay me back for the procedure."

"Want to show me how?"

"I would love to."

I rolled my eyes. He was being tactless, as usual, but he had a point: I had money now, and I didn't even know how much.

He walked me through the process of downloading a banking app and claiming my credentials. I logged in, and multiple accounts appeared—a checking, a savings, and some random investments. All of them had balances with several zeroes at the end, not that I had any appreciation for how much buying power that was. It had been a long time since I'd dealt with real money.

Nic showed me how to wire money to him. The amount he asked for barely put a dent in my checking.

"Stupid question," I asked as I scrolled through the transaction history. "But am I... rich?"

"Richer than I am," Nic muttered.

That didn't give me a whole lot to go on, but I still recognized that it wasn't a good thing. "Really?"

"The funny thing about being in the experimental sciences is that you're rarely working with your own money—you're usually investing someone else's. And thanks to Carnegie's fallout, I'm severely lacking in investors right now."

I swallowed. There was a lot I was worried about right now, but the stability of the base had never been one of them. Should I add it to the list?

"It will be fine," Nic said, not one to be pitied. "Now that I'm back in charge, I'll solicit new projects. But in the meantime, I might charge you rent."

I looked back down at the screen and tried to appreciate just how much I had. Apparently Thames had left me a great deal of money, and I tried to fathom, again, what had inspired a corrupt politician to want to adopt me and leave me an inheritance. According to the transaction history, he'd been paying into the account for over two years, which meant he'd been planning this since Ephesus went to Mars.

That's probably when he started watching you. I shuddered.

Nic got up from the table. "I'll slide the bill under your door on the first of each month."

I glanced up at him as he walked away. "So is it safe for me to go to town and buy stuff now?"

"You can buy whatever you want," he said without looking back. "Just make sure it's something Andromeda would own."

He left the cafeteria. I scarfed my cold, abandoned eggs and got up to find Mrs. Sardis.

There was one thing Andromeda needed.

4

The Martian city glittered under the light of a thousand artificial suns.

We'd gone to one of the newer settlements. It had been designed for tourists, and no expense had been spared to replicate the Martian dream. The streets were lined with neon, and every window flashed with electronic displays. The terrariums housed a freak circus of genetically modified plants that looked like they could be native to Mars. The walkways were covered with solid arches of glass wherever possible, so seamless and clear that you almost forgot you were inside. Adding to the illusion was the glow of daylight-replicating streetlamps. They augmented the distant sunlight and bathed the entire city in brightness, making everything look even more plastic and fake.

I'd asked Mrs. Sardis to take me clothes shopping, and she'd been delighted to oblige. I owned all of three outfits, none of which I could wear in public. Two I had worn while streaming, and the other—one of the skirts I had inherited from Mama—was so far out of fashion that it "screamed unassimilated," or so Mrs. Sardis claimed.

Fortunately, now that I had money, my wardrobe was an easy thing to rectify.

We'd gone to the shopping center first, but the pickings had been slim. There were only a few stores, each of which had but a dozen styles in limited sizes. Mrs. Sardis explained it was because it was so expensive to ship goods to Mars; even with the improvements in transit travel, flights were costly and depended wildly on Mars's rotation. During the wrong time of year, a flight from Earth could take twice as long and cost three times as much. That meant shipments of nonessential goods—like fashion—were infrequent and cost a premium.

Like everything else in the city, the clothing was designed to fulfill tourist fantasies, which meant most of it was more art than covering. I enjoyed browsing the shimmering array of vinyl and nylon but left without buying anything. Maybe I was being picky, but I didn't fancy looking like an alien from a bad movie, at least not for the prices they were charging.

Our next stop was proving much more fruitful—the thrift store. They called it an upscale rehoming boutique or some such nonsense, and the prices had an extra zero compared to the last thrift store I remembered from Earth, but it was still a vast improvement over the shopping center.

I found several pairs of jeans, including one with intentionally ripped-out knees. I wasn't too keen on pre-destructed clothing, but Mrs. Sardis said they were vintage enough to be cool again. I picked up a black leather jacket to replace my old pullover, plus new boots that weren't falling apart in the soles.

Meanwhile, Mrs. Sardis went to work finding shirts. It took a few "discussions" for us to settle on a new aesthetic for me. At first she wanted me to embrace the other end of the rainbow—pinks and neons and gaudy contrasting patterns. I would have preferred to stay in the safe realm of neutrals, but she reminded me that the whole purpose of our trip was to give myself a new look.

So we settled on a compromise—lots of black I could layer with colorful vests and scarves. She also picked out several t-shirts with benign graphics on them—abstract planets and stars, innocent pop bands, forgotten brand names.

But her most important find was a kitschy little black backpack to replace my well-worn pouch.

I took it from her and instantly hated it. It was stiff and bulky and plasticky—fake, just like Mars. It was nothing like the comforting leather satchel I was used to.

But then again, that was the point.

I added it to the pile with a sigh and went to check out.

Our next stop was a drug store to buy more makeup. Mrs. Sardis had done her best with foundation we'd borrowed from another lady on base, but I needed stuff that was my "shade," whatever that meant. Thankfully Mrs. Sardis knew what she was looking at, so I let her do the work and fill my basket with an assortment of creams and powders.

"Let's see, what's left?" she chatted as we loaded our haul into the car. "Oh, we should get you some jewelry. Have you thought about getting your ears pierced?"

I gaped at her. I was *exhausted*. I hadn't done this much shopping in six years, since before they sent us to the containment camps. Going to one more store sounded like torture, especially if it involved needles.

I'd had enough of those for one week.

She saw my face and laughed. "How about lunch, then?"

We retired to a café around the corner. Like everything else in the city, it was ridiculously themed, but at least the food was normal. I ordered soup and a fruity lemonade drink that was their special for the season, and Mrs. Sardis had an elaborate salad. We chatted about the weather and her son's antics and the newest arrivals on base—basically anything but what had gone on over the past month.

"Thanks for all your help today," I said as we were wrapping up. "I'd have been absolutely lost in that makeup department."

She chuckled. "When we get home, I'll show you how to use it. I promise it's not hard."

"If you say so." I smiled. Our waitress approached, and I flagged her down. "Here, let me pay. It's the least I can do."

"That's really not necessary, sweetheart. I'm happy to help." Mrs. Sardis reached into her purse, but I put my hand up.

"No, really. Apparently I can afford it, and besides, I'm still learning how to use this thing." I turned on my tablet and pulled up the universal payment app all United establishments were required to accept. The government had long since abandoned cash and card in favor of an app so that they could easily monitor and tax all transactions. Or at least that's how Nic explained it. My device sensed my location and automatically pulled up the café.

"How was everything?" Our waitress stopped at our table and claimed our dirty dishes. She was a spunky blonde thing that reminded me of a diminutive version of Cea, but with more tattoos.

"It was great. What's the total?" I looked her in the eyes and gave her a smile, which she returned.

"Oh, if you put your table number in here, it will pull it up for you." She leaned over my shoulder and pointed while I followed the motions. I tried not to be too fascinated by the technology—I'd nearly given myself away twice today by being amazed at things that Mrs. Sardis claimed were commonplace.

Spending five years in a containment camp will put you really far behind on technology.

"How do I add a tip? Do people still tip?" I realized how that must sound and faked a laugh. "I mean, I don't know how people do it on Mars."

I looked up at our waitress with what I hoped was a disarming smile and found her staring at me.

I was so unnerved that I returned the favor for a moment. Then I managed to clear my throat and ask, "Is that okay?"

She blinked and shifted back so she was no longer in my bubble. "I'm sorry, I mean… No, that total's not right. The system must not be syncing. I'll be right back." She snatched the rest of our dishes and hustled to the kitchen.

I watched her retreat, a brick settling in my stomach where lunch should have been. I glanced at the receipt displayed on the screen. "It looks right to me."

Mrs. Sardis shrugged and sipped the last of her iced tea. "Maybe something was on special."

If that was the case, our waitress was awfully upset about us being overcharged.

A stirring in my gut prodded me. *Leave. Now.*

But we haven't paid! I argued with Him, long enough that our waitress emerged from the back.

"Sorry about that. System's being dumb, so I had to print you a paper receipt." She laid a slip of white paper on the table. "Come again if you ever need anything."

I returned her gaze intentionally this time. She searched me for an almost indiscernible flicker, then turned to leave before I could thank her.

"I'm surprised they still have paper receipts," Mrs. Sardis commented.

I looked down at the slip, and my heart stopped.

Our meal had been comped—all the numbers replaced by zeros. At the bottom, on the line where a tip would have been, she'd scratched a single word:

#BLUEFIRE

I jerked my head up and searched for her, but she'd vanished.

I snatched the receipt and stuffed it in my pocket. "We need to get out of here."

Mrs. Sardis looked up from her phone. "What's wrong?"

I stood, trying to make the motion look casual, but my fingers shook as I gripped the table for balance. I strode towards the door as confidently as I could, hoping Mrs. Sardis would follow without making a scene. I cast a glance around at the other diners, looking for any prying eyes, but they all seemed absorbed in their own food and conversation.

I shoved the door open and hurried to the transfer. I keyed the code into the keypad and unlocked it from my side, jumping in and slamming the door before Mrs. Sardis even made it to the car.

"Phil, what's wrong?" she said as she opened the driver's door.

"It's Andi," I reminded her, "and just drive."

She obeyed. I didn't risk conversation until we'd cleared the border and were a good ten miles into the countryside, even though I realized that was paranoid. The transfer was built to contain its own atmosphere—no one was going to hear a hushed conversation through the thick glass.

But then again, no one was supposed to recognize me with my contacts and hair dye.

"Are you going to talk to me now?" Mrs. Sardis asked after she'd checked the rearview mirror to make sure we were alone in the wilderness.

I opened my mouth to answer—and suddenly realized I was having a full-blown panic attack. The pressure clogged my throat and shoved all cognitive thought out of my head except for blinding fear. I pulled the receipt out of my pocket and shoved it at her, then clenched my jaw to stop my teeth from chattering.

She drove with one hand while she smoothed the paper out and read it. She muttered something inaudible under her breath.

"Either she's seen my videos," I stuttered, words clipped, "or she heard about it from the tattoo artist."

Given the amount of ink she had on her arms, both scenarios were equally possible, and neither of them was good.

Mrs. Sardis stepped on the gas. "Nic will know what to do."

Will he? Nic couldn't fix this. At least two people now knew who I was—and, more importantly, that I was in this quadrant on Mars, which limited the search field significantly. How many other people they had told? If any of them recorded a video or made a social media post...

"Guess I should have gotten that piercing," I said, and sobbed.

Mrs. Sardis laid a consoling hand on my knee as she gunned the vehicle towards the base.

I'd never been so happy to see the glittering metal-and-glass structure rise on the horizon, even as I fought back the dread lining my stomach. How long would I be safe on base? One slip-up would turn my haven into a prison again—and bring Nic and everyone else down with me.

I was out of the car almost before the atmosphere was restored. The door to the lobby opened, revealing a tall figure posed there as if he had been waiting for us.

Nic. I was relieved to see him at the same time guilt nipped my cheeks. Had he already heard what happened?

I darted into the lobby and was about to spill my confession, but he spoke first.

"There's something you need to hear."

5

The recording was crackly and clogged with static, as if it had been ripped and modulated several times. His voice sounded close and yet muffled at the same time, and there was heavy background noise—maybe a train, or a car. But it was him.

"Radio check. This is Catalyst. Tell Blue Fire 10-4. Tell Klez 10-106. All listening 10-5. Over."

Daddy.

He repeated the message two more times, then the recording went silent. I stared at the blank media player on Nic's screen, letting the sound of my father's voice echo in my heart. I braced myself for a rush of emotion—the elation, the worry, the desire—but it never came. All I had was a tense longing, as if I were posed on the edge of a cliff, expecting—hoping—for more.

I looked down at Nic, who sat at the desk, watching me. "What did he mean?"

"10-4 means you've received and understood a message. So, assuming 'Blue Fire' means you…" Nic had the grace to soften his voice. "He's telling you he saw your videos."

There was the tidal wave of emotion as a dozen lonely, one-sided conversations suddenly came to fruition.

He knew. Daddy knew. He knew, and he understood.

Thank you, Jesus.

I swallowed back tears. "Any idea who Klez is?"

"It's an infamous computer virus from the 2000s, so best guess is it's your brother." Nic gestured at the screen. "10-106 means your status is secure. He's probably telling him it's safe to make contact."

My heart started beating faster as the implications took hold. "How did you get this recording?"

He hesitated for a suspicious beat. "From a... friend." He choked on the word, as if he wasn't sure he liked the taste. "He still monitors the CB down on Earth."

"The what now?"

"Citizens band—it's an old form of local radio."

"Radio," I repeated, and marveled.

Nic misinterpreted my silence. "Yes, it's a dated form of communicating sound over the electromagnetic spectrum—"

I put a hand up to stop him. "I know what a radio is. I just didn't think anyone used them anymore."

"They don't—not officially. Which is probably exactly why your father is." He leaned back in the chair. "The United banned most forms of radio because it's difficult to track. There are ways to find a transmitter, but only while it's actively broadcasting. More importantly, it's almost impossible to pinpoint the *receiver.* Not ideal for a government that wants a comprehensive log of its citizens' communication."

I pondered that. "So why aren't more people using it? People like us, I mean."

"Because it's horribly imprecise and utterly unsecured. If my friend picked up this transmission, that means anyone with a receiver in a five-mile radius heard it too—including the government."

I shuddered, but Nic generously assuaged my fears. "Unless your father left this broadcast running continually, they can't track him from it. All it tells them is what general vicinity he is—or was—in, and that's if they even realize who 'Catalyst' is."

"Did your friend know?"

Nic shrugged. "He was just doing what the message asked."

When I gave him a sideways look, he added, "10-5 means to relay the message."

"How do you know all this?"

"I looked it up."

I stared at the computer screen, a million hopes, plans, and prayers competing for priority in my mind. "Can we send him a message back?"

"You want to radio your father… *from Mars.*"

The pedantic tone of his voice told me everything I needed to know, but I didn't like being talked down to. "What? Radio waves travel that far. Right?"

"Oh distance isn't the problem," he grunted. "The problem is you have no way of telling him what channel you'll be on. That and the time delay with radio from up here is a bit tedious. But more important is the fact that you want to broadcast—from Mars—your identity, on a radio transmission that could be picked up by *literally* anyone."

"I get it, I get it." I sighed, and with that motion, the obvious solution settled into place. "Then I have to go back."

He didn't react, cold gray eyes searching mine. I repeated myself, mostly to anchor my own courage. "I have to go back to Earth."

"You actually don't," he returned.

I frowned at him. "Yes, I do. Dad's file is a mess—there's no way he could buy a transit ticket, even if I could make contact."

"Certainly not."

"And I know he doesn't have the money to forge a file."

"A reasonable assumption, but none of this necessitates that *you* have to go back to Earth." It was Nic's turn to sigh, like this whole thing was a necessary evil. "But I can see that you're going to."

I crossed my arms. "Do you have a better idea?"

"Several, including doing absolutely nothing." He turned back to the computer and started typing. "But what's your great idea?"

Well, it certainly doesn't involve sitting around doing nothing like you're doing. "I've got money, right?"

He grunted an affirmative.

"And you said it's easy to forge a file—maybe not one that looks legitimate, but at least enough of a shell to buy a transit ticket."

He glanced at the ceiling as if praying to some unknown god. "I did, unfortunately, say that."

"So if I can get back to Earth and make contact, I can buy him and Ephesus temp files and bring them back here."

I paused as the elephant in the room made its ungraceful appearance. "*Can* I bring them back here?"

"Well, let me think about that." His tone suggested he was actually giving it some thought, and I bit my lip. "If you bring your father and brother back here, I'll have all the loose cannons who could blow my cover under one roof where I can keep an eye on them. Yeah no—that sounds like a pretty good deal." He shot me a sideways glance. "Of course they can live here. Don't be petty. I'll even be nice and not force them to work against their will, since we're such good friends and all."

"Thanks," I said, trying to be genuine even though I wanted to slap him. "Where did your friend pick this up?" I gestured at the screen.

"Somewhere outside Boston."

"See? Dad hasn't even left the city—which means Ephesus probably hasn't either." Relief flushed through me as I ran the numbers. Thames's office was in Boston, which meant he had probably detained Dad and Ephesus somewhere nearby. Dad had stayed in the area to look for Ephesus, so Ephesus no doubt did the same. If they hadn't already made contact with each other, they soon would. All I had to do was go back to Earth and get them out.

I took a deep breath and straightened, the resolution solidifying in my stomach. "I'm going back."

Nic didn't look up, so I kept going. "I'm going back to find them and bring them home."

I mentally ran through the dozens of hitches to my plan. Radio wasn't private—I couldn't announce my identity and location on there any more than I could online. But I was currently on another *planet*, and Dad had still managed to make contact. If I could get down there and get within range, we could work together. I could save him and Ephesus. I had the money— and I even had the contacts.

"I'll call Jayde," I formulated my thoughts out loud. "He's got an altered file—he can hook me up with someone who can forge credentials for Dad and Ephesus. He can probably also get me a place to stay."

Nic stopped typing in the middle of a sentence and looked up. "You're going to do what?"

His tone made me second-guess everything that had left my mouth for the past five minutes. "I'm going back to Earth?"

"No, the next part."

"To find Dad and Ephesus and get them new files?"

"Keep going."

"And I'm staying with Jayde?"

He propped his arm over the back of the chair and regarded me. "I just need you to stop and appreciate the glorious stupidity of that statement."

"What?" I complained, although even as the word left my mouth, I realized how I must sound. It would sound less weird if everyone didn't have the annoying habit of calling Jayde my online boyfriend. "I won't stay with him *alone*, if that's what you're implying."

"Whether or not you have a chaperone is the least of my concerns," Nic scoffed. "What makes you think this is a good idea? No really," he said in response to my glare, "help me through your thought process. I'm learning how to communicate with a sheltered homeschooler."

I rolled my eyes at the same time I flushed red. "He's someone I trust—"

"Ahh! I'm going to stop you right there. That's your problem." Nic sat up and sketched in the air like he was writing on a whiteboard. "You see that word? Trust?" He spelled it out. "You're using it wrong. I don't think it means what you think it means."

I crossed my arms. "Oh? And what do *you* think it means?"

"Giving respect and access to someone who has proven themselves reliable," he said, which was a surprisingly biblical answer.

"Which Jayde has," I emphasized.

His eyebrows did their stupid little dance. "How so?"

"Did you miss the part where he saved us from Thames?"

"The way I see it, *you* saved us from Thames. But we can argue about how many star stickers you both get on your achievement charts later. The point is, you can't trust Jayde."

I trust him more than I trust you, I thought, and unfortunately the sentiment came out in words. "And what would you know about trust?"

He was unaffected. "I trust you."

I stopped.

"Look, I know he's cute and heroic and all, but you shouldn't trust him. Thank him if you must, but don't give him any slack. Whatever you think you're feeling, it ain't trust."

Then what is it? I challenged, and searched my spirit. I had no reason not to trust Jayde. He had been kind to me; he'd helped me break out of jail; he'd given me valuable information; and he'd helped me stop Thames. He'd never done anything to betray my trust. What more was I looking for?

Nic tried to help. "You don't *know* him, Andi. You realize that, right?" His tone suggested that he doubted my mental capacity to complete this self-assessment.

I met his gaze. "What do you mean? I met him when Thames arrested me."

"Yeah, but you have no idea if this is the same guy. Have you talked on the phone? Video chatted? No, you haven't. He could literally be anybody."

The realization that he was right dawned on me with a shiver that crawled up my spine. "But he knew my nicknames, and about Cea..."

"So did Carnegie."

I flinched.

Immediately, I started second-guessing every interaction I'd had with "Aurelius." What if it *wasn't* Jayde? Who else could it be? He acted like my friend, sure—but even Thames had pretended like he cared about me. What if I *couldn't* trust him?

But then, how did "Aurelius" know so much about Jayde? He'd known about the incident with Cea, and Jayde's job, and his security access. If it wasn't Jayde talking, the only other explanation was that "Aurelius" had done something *to* Jayde.

That was an extreme scenario, of course, but Nic was right. I didn't know. I didn't know anything. *Oh God, what have I done?*

Nic seemed uninterested in my self-flagellation. "If he's being helpful or offering useful information, take advantage of that. But if you want my advice?"

He paused. I waited. I did want it, but I wasn't going to beg for it.

Nic turned back to his computer. "Use him, but don't trust him."

He resumed typing while I marinated that admonition in silence. He was right—traveling *to another planet* to stay with a stranger wasn't my smartest idea, especially when I had a secret identity to protect.

"But I still need to get back to Earth," I continued the thought aloud.

"That's one solution," he said without looking up.

"Which means I need a place to stay."

"You've got money—book a hotel."

I did have the money, but staying in a hotel didn't sound much safer than meeting up with Jayde. Everyone saw you come and go at a hotel; if I was trying to slide under the radar, checking into public accommodations that were heavily surveilled was probably not my best option.

"You got any better ideas?" I shot back.

He stopped typing and stared at the wall for a minute.

"Well." He punched a key to end whatever he was doing on the computer. "You could stay with my parents."

6

Nic waited patiently for me to adjust my reality around that statement.

I cleared my throat. "So, this is going to sound dumb…"

"I'm used to it."

"…because I realize, factually speaking, everyone has parents…"

"That is how biology works."

"…but I didn't realize you, you know, *had* parents."

"You thought they were dead," he said patronizingly, like he was bargaining with a five-year-old.

"Yeah. And don't say I never asked." I cut him off with a finger wag. "Because when would we have had time to talk about that?"

"Exactly. My familial status has been completely irrelevant up until this present moment. Now that this information potentially has some value to you, I'm offering it."

"Thanks." Had it only been Nic involved, I would have accepted that explanation and moved on. However, Nic was not an only child. "Cea acts like your parents are dead."

"To her, they are."

The most likely conclusion washed over my nerves like liquid nitrogen. "Does she… know they're alive?"

For the first time since we'd met, Nic made the effort to look properly offended. "Of course she knows. What, you think I'd lie about that?"

"Wouldn't be the first time you faked somebody's death," I mumbled.

He paused to consider that. "Fair point, although I think your limited experience skews the data. But no." He leveled his voice, the one reliable marker of his intentionality. "She knows. She just decided it was easier to pretend they were dead than to contend with the uncomfortable reality of their existence."

"Why?"

"Coping mechanism. Yours is obsessive-compulsive reading. Hers is avoiding confrontation."

"No, I mean like, what happened?"

Nic sighed and rapped his finger on the desk, and I suddenly realized that Cea wasn't the only one avoiding things.

"They had neurosurgery," he declared finally.

I swallowed. "Why?"

He frowned. "You've met my sister—why do you think?"

I thought about the illegal Bibles Nic had on his database and smiled. "They're Christian."

"*Were,*" Nic corrected, not returning my smile.

I searched his expression. "When did they undergo the procedure?"

"About eight years ago."

I did the math. Cea would have still been a teenager. More importantly, that was before neurosurgery had been deemed "safe."

I wasn't sure the procedure had ever gotten full federal approval as a legal corrective device. They talked about it periodically; usually it came up around election time to give the career politicians something polarizing but irrelevant to debate on TV. It had been a long time since I'd heard of anyone undergoing the procedure; the containment camps were a much more palatable option for reconditioning unassimilated people like me.

Nic wasn't volunteering any more information, so I knew I'd have to lead. "But they survived?"

"With flying colors—if you consider only their physical health. It could have been the celebrity case that inspired the legalization of the procedure, if it weren't for the annoying complication that they both forgot literally everything they know."

He glared at the unforgiving wall of his office. I gave him space and waited.

"Dad was an engineer. Brilliant—way more than me. The experiments I've done look like science fair projects compared to what he's accomplished."

That seemed like a stretch—considering the numerous diabolical heists Nic had pulled off—but maybe he was better at scheming than engineering. Still, it was the most endearing thing I'd ever heard him say about another human being.

"He helped designed stations like this." Nic waved his hand at the glass-and-metal dome that shielded us from the sparse Martian atmosphere. "He was one of the main scientists responsible for putting humans on Mars."

I gave that achievement the moment of silence it deserved. "Why would they risk putting someone like that through neurosurgery? That seems self-defeating."

"That's what I said. But you know how legalistic they are. Having your top-awarded scientist be unassimilated doesn't look good on press releases. I guess they were hoping they could cut the saint out of his brain but keep the doctor."

I knew exactly how the United was—but neurosurgery still seemed like a ridiculously ineffective solution to the problem. "Couldn't they have just locked him up in a containment camp and forced him to work for free?"

"Those weren't public knowledge yet—but believe me, they tried. Dad wouldn't have it and raised all hell." Nic regarded me with something that could almost be construed as affection. "You two would have gotten along."

I smiled, but that was as far as the sentiment went for Nic. His face returned to its natural state of condescension as he continued, "Dad never took no for an answer either—put him in a containment camp and he'd blow the place up. Which he did. Twice."

"I think I heard about that." I had vague recollections of seeing it on the news and overhearing Mom and Dad talk about it when they thought I wasn't listening. Of course, the news had vaguely referred to the camp as a "correctional facility"; I had no idea I'd be living in one a few years later.

"You probably did—he was too high-profile to keep out of the news. Eventually he told them that they'd have to put a bullet in his head if they wanted him to deny his religion, and Mom was right there with him. No amount of pleading from me *or* Cea could convince them otherwise."

I stiffened. "So they put them under?"

"Without consent or warning. I didn't get the call until the state realized they needed 24/7 care. Thought they could rope me into doing it for free because we're 'family.' I told them I was current on my taxes."

I imagined that was *not* what Nic had said to them, but I was grateful to him for not repeating the actual language he used. "They're braindead?" I reached the obvious conclusion.

"Oh no, their brains are functioning perfectly. They've just been wiped of any useful information."

I searched his face for any residue of emotion. "They don't remember you."

"Or any of their combined five doctorate degrees, or how to function in polite society, or how to survive as independent adults. They're doing better now, but it took almost three years of therapy and round-the-clock care to get them to the point where they could largely take care of themselves. Ever try to potty-train a forty-year-old?"

I cringed. If the bad PR wasn't enough to kill the legalization of neurosurgery, the fact that it ladened the state with costly dependents no doubt doomed it. It was cheaper to put people in a work camp—or kill them, if you were willing to deal with the paperwork.

"I'm sorry," was all I could think of to say, and it seemed the most inadequate.

Nic shrugged and sank in his chair, as if the emotional transparency had exhausted him.

I gave him a minute to recover. It certainly explained why Nic hated the United—although I'm sure there had been more than one grudge motivating his mastermind plan to cut Mars off from government control. And Cea—I was still surprised she hadn't said anything to me, especially after I'd been so frank about my own mother's death. But I could see why it was easier for her to pretend they were gone.

Sometimes it's easier to pretend people aren't there than to wish for a relationship you can't have.

I prayed for Cea, wherever she was, and then my present conundrum regained control of my thoughts. How did any of this help me in my search for a place to stay?

"Is it safe for me to stay with them?"

Nic barked a dry laugh. "Their house is probably the safest place on Earth. They're completely harmless and intolerably dull, and they'll forget you as soon as you leave the room." His eyes finally met mine. "Which for you is a big plus."

It would definitely be in my favor to stay with someone who couldn't tell the United—or Carnegie—where I'd been.

"Besides," Nic continued, "since I'm your legal guardian, no one will question why I sent you to visit my parents. So if anyone does happen to check your papers, it will make sense."

I nodded, convinced. "Okay."

Nic returned the gesture. "I'll make some calls." He resumed typing. "Mom might give you a hard time, but don't let her bully you."

I decided to avoid the obvious sarcastic response. "How do I buy a ticket back to Earth?"

"Ask Sardis."

"You don't know how?"

"No, I just don't want to help you with something so pedestrian. That's why I have people. Tell Sardis what you're doing, and he'll take care of everything. Just let me know when you leave the planet."

"Okay. And thank you." He didn't acknowledge that, so I turned to go.

"Andromeda."

I glanced back at him, expecting a heartless goodbye.

He didn't look up from his screen. "Tell my folks I said hi."

7

Three hours later, I had my transit ticket.

We could have accomplished it much sooner had the Sardises not spent the first hour trying to talk me out of going, and then the next hour and a half scouring the internet trying to find the best deal on a flight. I told them I had enough money—I could just buy direct from the transit line—but Mr. Sardis insisted on finding a discount. After we found one that satisfied his budget—and my itinerary—Mrs. Sardis walked me back to my dorm and helped me pack.

I couldn't take any of my old outfits, that was a given. I thought about throwing everything away, but Mrs. Sardis suggested I hang them in the back of the closet so I could have them "if" I came back.

She did not say "when."

She watched me as I folded my suite of unworn jeans and t-shirts into a carryon she'd loaned me. It was too risky to take Mama's purple suitcase—Carnegie was the only person alive who knew what it looked like, but he was one of the main people I didn't want to find me.

"Are you sure about this?" she said after several minutes of silence.

It was no use answering the question for the tenth time that night, so instead I returned with, "Do you think I shouldn't?"

Her sigh said everything. "What about Carnegie? We have no idea where he is. What if he's watching the base and follows you out there?"

That seemed unlikely. Nic had more than one layer of security around the base, and according to the proximity sensors, Carnegie had left when Thames died and not returned. It was far more likely that the cunning old man had fled to Earth to regroup and find new investors, but his file hadn't been updated one way or the other in the past two weeks. It wasn't out of the realm of possibility that he was still around.

But no matter where he was, I knew Carnegie was also after my father—and I couldn't let him get there first. "I have to find my dad before Carnegie does. Besides, if Ephesus and Cea are alive, they're probably still in the area. They may have heard Dad's message too."

I was fully aware of how many "if's" I'd crammed into that breath, but it didn't matter. Nothing she could say would have convinced me to stay. I had an opportunity to find my family, and I was taking it.

"But what if someone recognizes you?" She must have realized I wasn't responding to "what if's," because she abruptly changed tactics. "Someone *will* recognize you. Someone recognized you today—on Mars, where there *isn't* a security camera on every corner."

I looked up and caught my reflection in the mirrored closet doors. She had a point. The waitress today may have been tipped off, but millions of people on Earth had seen my videos. And that didn't count the dozens of United officials who were actively searching for me and my father.

Mars wasn't looking for me. Earth was.

I straightened and ran a hand over my hair, which was sticky and shiny from the cheap dye. I was still wearing my contacts and makeup from before, and even I could see that the façade only ran skin deep. Between my greasy hair and cakey foundation, I *looked* fake.

And if I was going to find my father before our enemies did, spending two hours in the bathroom every day putting on my face was probably not to my advantage.

But what else could I do? I'd tried everything to hide my appearance—everything that wasn't permanent.

My courage choked in my throat. Nic's angry words echoed back to me.

That girl is dead to you.

I pinched a chunk of hair between my fingers.

Let her die.

Mrs. Sardis mistook my silence. "Please, Philadelphia, reconsider."

I strode over to the desk before I could do exactly that. I threw the drawers open with a bang, rooting through the standard-issue tape and glue until I found what I was looking for: a pair of scissors.

I turned back to the mirror and held the scissors close to my ear. A flash of panic almost stopped me—that was ten years of growth I held in my fist.

Mrs. Sardis cautiously stood up. "Philadelphia…?"

I tightened my grip. "My name is Andromeda Nolan."

I slid the scissors down until they were just past my shoulder, closed my eyes, and cut.

Mrs. Sardis gasped.

I dropped the dead hair on the floor. I gave my heart a minute to calm down before I opened my eyes and turned to face her.

"How do you think I would look blonde?"

*

By morning, I was unrecognizable.

After Mrs. Sardis had cried over my cut locks and fussed about how I didn't have to do that—even though we both knew I definitely did—she ran to find someone to "fix" it. With the help of the lab techs and their chemicals, we bleached my hair to an ashy shade of blonde, and Mrs. Sardis tidied my hack job. My hair now fell just to my shoulders.

I'd also taken Mrs. Sardis's suggestion and gotten my ears pierced. Again, the techs had more than enough implements that could put a hole in my ear, so I got one stud on my left ear and two on my right. Mrs. Sardis said asymmetrical piercings were all the rage on Earth right now.

I had to admit, it matched the rest of my new aesthetic: ripped jeans, black jacket, generic band t-shirt. I switched my green contacts for a haunting blue and painted my nails an arrogant shade of purple. I'd gone lighter on the makeup, aiming for a look that was more natural, with a brush of bronzer to make it look like I'd seen Earth's sun in the last decade.

I spun before the mirror and tried to tell myself that I liked my appearance. I looked good—cohesive, convincing, like I was a real person. But something was missing.

I walked to my suitcase that lay open on the coffee table and rooted through my makeup bag. My fingers closed around a thin object. I pulled it out and held it up to the light: the mascara Narissa had given me. Her note was still taped to the end.

I twirled it in my fingers and tried to picture how she had done my makeup. There had been a lot more steps involved—more than I would ever be able to master on my own—but surely I could copy some of it.

I grabbed a black eyeliner and turned back to the mirror. Taking a deep breath to steady my hand, I drew a thin line under each eye. Then I found the eyeshadow palette Mrs. Sardis had picked out and painted my lids a murky purple with a hint of glitter.

I stood back and looked myself over again. The illusion was perfect. I looked moody, confident, calm.

Everything I wasn't feeling right now.

Swallowing a prayer, I sat down on the couch and picked up my tablet. The screen flickered on to a barrage of notifications. "Aurelius," as he often did, had sent me a tsunami of texts.

I'd messaged him briefly yesterday to give him my new username and apologize for Nic; mercifully, he'd taken the whole thing in stride. But in all the chaos of last night, I'd forgotten to check my messages until just now, and he had assumed the worst of my absence.

I skimmed the message history. It was clear he had also heard about Dad's transmission, which confirmed a couple of things. One, that the underground was still monitoring "the CB," and two, that people had obeyed the message and passed it along. That meant it was very likely Cea and Ephesus had heard it, if they were still in the area—but it also meant that Carnegie and the United officials had heard it.

This is why I have to get down there now.

I kept reading. I could tell when Aurelius's messages changed from friendly prods to concerned questions, concern that had gotten increasingly more frantic when I'd failed to respond.

It did look like he had taken Nic's warning to heart, though, because his messages were noticeably absent of names. Instead, he tried every way to tell me, without telling me, that he'd heard my father's transmission and was wondering what I was going to do.

HEARD THE NEWS. WHAT DO YOU THINK?

ARE YOU COMING TO THE PARTY?

SRSLY CHECK YOUR TEXTS

HEY. NEED TO KNOW IF YOU'RE COMING

EVERYTHING GOOD? ANYTHING I SHOULD KNOW?

I clicked in the text box and stared at the blinking cursor, writing and rewriting my reply in my head. How could I tell him discretely that I was on my way to Earth?

You don't know him.

I took my hand away from the keyboard. I didn't know Jayde—but then again, I didn't know anybody. I had no one. Everyone I used to know was either locked in a containment camp or on the run. I was going to walk into one of the United's biggest metropolitan areas, armed with a fake identity and some eyeliner, to stay with strangers who had been brain-wiped.

It would be nice to have an ally who had all his faculties.

He could literally be anybody.

But then again, I still had no idea why Jayde—if it was him—had even befriended me. All I knew was that he hated the United, at least enough to help me fight Thames. But how deep did that loyalty run? What skin did he have in this game? He had gone to an awful lot of effort and put himself at great risk for someone he'd only known for a few weeks. Why?

And in the meantime, he was also the dead man's switch on the bomb that was my new identity. He was the only person outside the base who knew my real name and had a way to contact me. He could reveal my location to anyone—and if he saw me in person, with my new hair and style, he could tell the United everything they needed to know.

Use him, but don't trust him.

Nic was right; Aurelius couldn't know I was on Earth.

I pondered sending a goodbye message but thought better of it. I closed the app before I could change my mind, turned my tablet off, and zipped it in my backpack.

Mr. Sardis met me in the docking bay. He hadn't seen me since yesterday, so he took in my new appearance with a wide-eyed stare. "You look great," he said finally, but I couldn't tell if he meant it. "Ready to go?"

There was a fake pause and even faker smile that punctuated that statement, and I knew that was a final plea for me to change my mind. I didn't trust my voice to be confident, so I just nodded firmly and handed him my suitcase.

He sighed and loaded it in the trunk.

A voice emerged from behind us. "When will you be back?"

I turned to see Nic standing in the doorway to the lobby. "Me?" I asked, and panicked. I had no idea when I would be back; I hadn't even stopped to consider it.

Nic shook his head and gestured at Mr. Sardis. "I expect about four hours, sir," he answered. "I'd like to see her off if you can spare me."

Nic nodded. Mr. Sardis tipped an imaginary hat and climbed into the driver's seat.

Nic reached into the pocket of his lab coat and withdrew a white business card. He wordlessly held it out to me. I took it and squinted at the small print. There was nothing on it except for a graphic of a mountain range and a phone number with a country code I didn't recognize. I looked up at him and raised an eyebrow.

"Don't call him until you're ready to buy new files," he said. "But when you do, tell him I sent you."

I nodded and slid the card into the inner pocket of my backpack. Then I walked to the transfer and opened the passenger door.

"Philadelphia," he called.

I glanced back at him, startled that he'd used my real name.

His eyes found mine. His voice held no ambiguity as he said, "Keep your head down."

Then before I could respond, he stepped back into the lobby and shut the door.

8

I stopped in the middle of the sidewalk and put on a great show of looking like I knew what I was doing.

The flight down had been uneventful. Mr. Sardis had carried my luggage to security, bought me a bag of candy for the ride, and given me a long, fatherly hug that I savored. Then he mercifully let me go without another word.

I'd given myself a little scare when I scanned my fingerprints and *Nolan, Andromeda* popped up on my ticket. That's what it was supposed to say, of course, but it was still weird seeing it in print.

I'd gathered my wits and passed through security without an issue. There were no glitches, no warnings on my file, and no wary glances from strangers. One of the attendants even complimented my asymmetrical piercing. Then I was ushered to my seat and left to my own devices.

I managed the three-day flight just fine—it wasn't the first time I'd made the trip—and even succeeded in navigating the labyrinthian transit hub in Boston to pick up my luggage. I found my way outside to the bus stop, and that was where my confidence ground to a halt.

I stood on the curb and was assaulted with the blare of car horns, the roar of launching airplanes, the throbbing of a crowd of people, and the crippling realization that this was the first time I'd been "outside" in nearly six years.

Unless you counted my brief stint in Stanyard's basement, I'd spent my entire teenage years either locked in a containment camp, fighting for my life in jail, or secluded on the base on Mars. None of which had done anything to prepare me for the challenge of navigating Boston's public transportation system.

In retrospect, I probably should have done some research on basic life skills—how to ride the bus, how to buy groceries, what music was trending—because right now, my greatest enemy was my ignorance. My official file now claimed I had nearly eighteen years of well-adjusted life experience, and the world was going to expect me to act like it.

I took a deep breath and let it out with a prayer. The Holy Spirit had gotten me out of a burning factory, among other inconceivable scrapes—surely He could help me figure out the bus.

I took my tablet out of my backpack. I typed the address Nic had given me into maps and routed walking directions. The internet rose to the occasion and populated a step-by-step path.

I laughed to myself. One benefit of living in a hyper-connected and heavily-surveilled economy was that you could give very precise directions.

I checked the digital signboard and found the bus I needed. The next one was due in mere minutes, so I shouldered my carryon and ran the rest of the way. I made it just as the bus jerked up to the curb, its electric engine buzzing at an annoying pitch. I joined the short line of people waiting to board and watched their motions.

The first two simply walked onto the bus without even glancing at the driver. A bar above the door chirped and flashed green as they passed.

The next man attempted to board, but the door flashed red and screeched at him. I reflexively cringed, the nightmare of a hundred rejections rushing back at me. The driver glanced up and gave the man a bored stare. The man grumbled, took off his overstuffed backpack, and rooted through it until he found a laptop. He made a dramatic scene of holding it up to the scanner, which accepted the sacrifice and turned green. The man continued to mutter as he dragged his backpack to a seat in the rear.

Then it was my turn. I panicked, even as my feet continued to move me forward. What if I needed a special app?

Too late to ask. I put my foot on the step and braced myself for the denial and shame—but the bus welcomed me warmly. The driver acknowledged me with a jerk of his thumb towards the back, and I stumbled to an empty seat, trying not to shake with relief. I sat down just as the bus lurched forward.

There, I told myself and the Holy Spirit. *One step done.*

I would be riding this bus for a while—the first stop was a transfer hub twenty minutes away—so I settled back in the seat and watched out the window. Boston had been my city all my life, but I rarely got to see it like this.

It was approaching six o'clock, and the world was caught in the twilight. The sun was just beginning to set, but the streetlights had not yet turned on, so the city was bathed in soft glow and shadow. Rush hour had given way to the post-dinner stroll. People—beautiful, disparate, unique people—milled on sidewalks and crowded taverns. A few children still played in parks and chased electric scooters down the sidewalk. The scenery was both welcoming and foreign at the same time.

With my anxiety pacified, my consciousness had room for curiosity. If there wasn't a special app, how did the bus know I was cleared to ride? I knew there was no ticket fee—they'd taught us that much in school—but the door had scanned *something.*

I pulled out my tablet and flipped through my recent notifications. There was a location ping stating that I'd boarded bus #763 at stop 1112 for the westbound 64 route. I clicked on the notification, and it pulled up my personal file.

There I was, Andromeda Nolan, with all my recent travel activity dutifully logged. Since I owned this file, I could see every piece of information that was associated with my name—at least, every piece of information the United wanted me to see.

It made you wonder how much information the United was recording that they didn't disclose.

But how did the bus know it was me? The only explanation was that it had scanned my tablet—which was now officially registered as belonging to Andromeda Nolan.

I thought back to the warnings Nic had given me before I left. Between him and Mr. Sardis—who had given me a safety lecture on the ride to the transit hub—I'd compiled a lengthy list of rules for my trip.

Rule 1: Remember that any time you make an electronic transaction or pass under a censor bar, you're making a permanent log under Andromeda. Don't do anything or go anywhere that she wouldn't.

Well, if anyone was watching Andromeda's file, they now knew she was back on Earth. It was that sinisterly simple—all I had to do was board a bus, and the United knew exactly where I was and where I was going, if they cared to look.

I shuddered, but there was no avoiding it, so I packed the feeling down and tried to ignore it. No one was looking at my file. The trick was to keep it that way.

It was nearly dark by the time I'd transferred buses and gotten off in a ritzy subdivision in Allston. The houses weren't large—most of them were hardly bigger than the concrete boxes we'd had in the containment camp—but they were single-family, which for downtown was a luxury. The homes were tall and narrow, with barely a hair's breadth of yard between them. Most of them had been built in the 1900s, and even though they had been plastered over with metal siding and solar panels, their age showed. Far nicer (and larger) condos could have been obtained at a fraction of the cost, but apparently the privilege of genetically modified grass was worth paying for.

Nic's parents lived in a house at the end of the street. Their porchlight wasn't on, but I wasn't expecting it to be. Nic said he'd called to let them know I was coming, but he also said they would likely forget as soon as they hung up the phone.

In other words, I was calling on this poor couple unannounced, expecting to be given a place to stay.

And I absolutely did not have a backup plan if they refused.

I took a deep breath. *Holy Spirit, pave the way.*

I walked up to the door and waved my hand over the touchless doorbell. The words "please wait" danced across the screen. The admonition was moot, because the door opened not ten seconds later.

A quaint elderly couple appeared in the doorway, backlit by the warm glow of their living room lamps. They looked so perfect and kind and stereotyped that it was easier to imagine them as characters in a TV show than as real people. Even their motions seemed scripted as the wife pulled open the door, her husband calling *"Who is it, honey?"* as he approached from behind.

I answered before either of them could ask. "Hi, Mrs. Von Nieuwenhuyse. I'm Andromeda Nolan. Nic sent me—he said he called."

Roseanne—Nic had mercifully given me a rundown of their names—opened the storm door but didn't step out onto the porch. She was a more elegant, refined version of Cea, her graying curls styled primly around her contoured face. Her eyes were piercing, and she gave me a once-over so sharp that I'm surprised the motion didn't give her whiplash. "Who are you? And who's Nic?"

I swallowed as I remembered Nic's second rule.

Rule 2: Don't try to explain to my parents that they have a son. You'll get stuck in that conversation forever. Just tell them I'm a colleague of his and we used to work together.

"He worked with you after college." I turned my attention to Paul, who was crowding his wife's shoulder in the doorway. "You were partners in a big space station project."

"Really?" Paul mused, but he sounded more like he was fascinated by the idea than recognizing that it belonged to him. He looked like a police sketch of Nic aged thirty years. He had a nearly identical fluffy mustache with an afterthought of a goatee. Both were washed a comforting salt-and-pepper gray, but his wayward hair still had a bit of blond left in it.

Roseanne glanced back at him. "Space stations? Since when have you worked on space stations?"

"I've been working on space stations since…" Paul started, then realized he had no idea.

I tried to grab the conversation and reel it back in. "I just came from a Martian base you helped design," I boasted—which, according to Nic, was essentially the truth. "It's an honor to meet you."

"Mars!" he crowed. "I've always wanted to see Mars."

"That's news to me," Roseanne muttered.

Paul either didn't hear her or chose to ignore her. He gave me a second look, as if I had suddenly gotten far more interesting. "You live up there? Maybe I should come visit you on my next vacation."

I imagined the Von Nieuwenhuyses visiting their son on Mars and couldn't decide if that would be endearing or disastrous. "Nic would love to have you. He spoke very highly of you."

"Oh, did he now?" Paul's eyes twinkled, and I knew I'd won him over.

I returned his grin. "He has the utmost respect for you and your work, and he wanted me to tell you he says hello."

Paul looked positively tickled, but Roseanne hadn't caught up yet. "He sent you all the way from Mars just to tell us that? Does he know emails exist?"

Her tone could have cut sheetrock, and I suddenly realized which parent Nic took after.

Also just like Nic, her sharpness made me falter and question everything about myself. "No, I… he suggested you would be a safe place to stay while I… applied to Harvard." That was the story Nic had told me to repeat, but it suddenly sounded lame to my ears.

"Good luck getting in there," she huffed. "And this man, Nic, he's your… father?"

"Ew no," I said, too quickly. "I'm his…" *What am I?* I stalled, then settled for a partial truth. "My parents used to work for him. He took me in when they died."

The light in Paul's eyes flickered like a threatened candle. "I'm very sorry to hear that, dear, but it sounds like you're in good hands. He must be a very kind man."

When he wants to be.

My tragic backstory did seem to soften Roseanne a bit. "Yes, a very kind thing of him to do. I'm sure his parents are proud. But I'm just not sure we're set up to accommodate guests right now." She glanced up at her husband, silently prodding him to verify her statement.

I jumped in before he could answer. "I can cook and clean. I won't be any trouble."

Even as the word left my mouth, I imagined Nic laughing doubtfully.

The mention of food distracted Paul from the silent signals his wife was sending him. "Well now, that sounds like a pretty good deal!"

Roseanne dropped her pretense of subtlety. "Paul! We can't just invite strangers into our home!"

"I'm not—" I started, but Paul was quicker on the draw.

"She's not a stranger! She's a friend of Nic's. Besides, we can't turn her away now—it's late."

"It's 6pm," she deadpanned.

Paul was already walking back into the house, waving at me to follow. "Come on, it's cold out."

Roseanne made a last-ditch effort, even as she stepped out of the way to let me pass. "It's sixty-five degrees!"

"Well, I'm cold!"

She sighed, then frowned down at me. I picked up my carryon and found my most charming smile. "Thank you, Mrs. Von."

Rule 3: Don't waste your breath calling them Mr. and Mrs. Von Nieuwenhuyse. Mr. and Mrs. Von is just fine.

"Should I start calling you Dr. Von Nieuwenhuyse?"

"Not unless you want to be put up for adoption."

Mrs. Von offered me a smile that was about as genuine as most of Nic's, but she did let me in.

Mr. Von must have taken me literally on my offer to cook, because before I could even shed my jacket, he was showing me around the kitchen and asking me what we should make with the ground beef they had thawed. I could tell by the various implements and spices that were out on the counter that Mrs. Von had already started something—although whether or not she remembered what she was cooking was another story. I didn't want to step on her toes more than I already had, so I deferred and instead offered to wash the dishes.

Dinner was a production. It involved me reintroducing myself twice (to each of them on separate occasions), and I'm pretty sure the dish we ended up with was not the one Mrs. Von had intended to make when she started. But it was edible, and the comforting camaraderie of sitting around a dining room table with a family was worth the hassle.

Mrs. Von was more than happy to let me do all the cleanup as penance for my imposition, and by the time I was done, they'd both retired to the living room in front of the TV and completely forgotten about me. I bid them goodnight to a chorus of vague "Yes dear's" and went to show myself around the house.

There were two unused bedrooms on the second floor. Both of them had been shut up for years and, as such, had been spared the misery of forgetfulness. Unlike the rest of the house, which had been edited and rearranged by a woman who didn't know who she was, these bedrooms had been sealed like a time capsule, with Nic and Cea's childhood embalmed within.

Nic had the bedroom on the left. It was almost as austere and undecorated as the man himself, but the air of studiousness was as thick as the layer of dust that had settled on the furniture. The carpet near the wall was indented with the ghosts of overladen bookcases. There was a large desk, an even larger drafting board, and an advanced telescope that had, in its day, been top-of-the-line. All of it was arranged with exacting precision like hands on a clock.

Cea's bedroom was on the right. It gave the impression that she had attempted to be a girly girl in high school and then never bothered to change her wallpaper, even as her aesthetic drifted in another direction. A guitar with a snapped neck—signed by some emo heartbreaker—had been mounted on the wall right over pink psychedelic decals with curling edges. Memorabilia for bands from the previous decade competed with dolls and decaying makeup compacts on the dresser. And scattered here and there were trophies from her stint as a cheerleader—a signed jersey, dusty pompoms, and a frilled uniform hiding in the back of the closet.

I tried to imagine Cea in a short skirt performing somersaults on a football field, but I couldn't reconcile that image with the sharpshooter I knew now. I supposed that cheerleader didn't exist anymore, just like her parents, who were downstairs wandering lost in their own living room.

I decided it was more appropriate that I stay in Cea's room, even though Nic's felt strangely more familiar. I debated leaving my clothes in my suitcase—how long would I be staying?—but realized it would look better if I put on a pretense of settling in. I shoved Cea's old outfits to the side and hung mine up in the closet, arranged my makeup on the dresser, and set up the charging dock for my tablet on the nightstand, right next to a highschool-era picture of Nic and Cea that I was sure I'd seen hanging somewhere on base.

After I dismantled my hair and makeup, I settled on the bed and turned on my tablet.

Aurelius had sent numerous messages, all of which were variously-worded pleas begging me to respond—as he had been doing for the past five days. I cleared the notifications and ignored them, even though my heart twinged a little when I did it. Then I switched over and read the text from Nic.

DID THEY LET YOU IN THE DOOR?

NOT FOR LACK OF TRYING ON YOUR MOM'S PART

I WARNED YOU

YOU UNDERSOLD IT. EVEN YOU'RE MORE FRIENDLY THAN SHE IS

He didn't respond, which either meant I'd gone too far, or he didn't want to admit that he did, in fact, know how to be nice to me. I attempted to salvage the conversation.

THANKS AGAIN FOR THE HELP

JUST REMEMBER IT TAKES LIKE 5 MINUTES FOR THE WATER TO RUN HOT IN THE UPSTAIRS SHOWER

I acknowledged that with a thumbs up, and he went offline. I closed the app and was suddenly reminded that I was very much alone on Earth.

The basket cases downstairs hardly counted.

And now what? I had gotten in the door and secured a safe place to stay—at least until they forgot about me and called the cops on their home intruder—but now I had to come up with a plan to find my dad, the most wanted man in the district. All without blowing my cover and ruining Andromeda's spotless reputation.

I picked Nic and Cea's picture off the nightstand. I tapped the glass over their stoic faces and wondered, not for the first time, how much easier this would be if either of them was here.

I set the picture down on the nightstand, flopped back on the pillow, and picked up my tablet. I reflexively went to open my Bible reader—then hesitated.

Rule 4: Remember that the Bible is illegal media, so take your reader offline if you're going to read it. But also remember that offline devices are illegal, so use them sparingly.

I glanced at the clock; it was late enough that nobody would expect me to be online. The algorithm better get used to the fact that Andromeda went to "bed" early every night.

I took my device offline, opened my reader, and started a conversation with the one person I knew wouldn't leave me.

9

The smell of bacon burning drew me out of sleep before my alarm did. I lay there, staring at the faded unicorn sticker preteen Cea had stuck to her ceiling fan, and waited until I heard Mrs. Von cussing herself out in the kitchen before I got up.

I sat on the edge of the bed and brought my tablet back online. My messaging app nearly choked on itself as it chimed multiple notifications at once. I knew without looking who it was; Aurelius had sent his usual barrage of angsty good mornings.

I sighed, managing to feel annoyed and guilty in equal proportions. Would it hurt just to let him know I was okay? I could at least tell him that I was safe; he didn't need to know anything else.

I opened the chat. Nic had showed me how to turn off the feature that let the sender know I'd read the message, so I could skim the notifications in private.

I TAKE IT YOU'RE NOT COMING TO THE PARTY.
ANY REASON WHY?

EVERYONE'S ASKING ABOUT YOU. THEY WANT TO KNOW IF YOU'RE COMING. DO YOU NEED A RIDE?

IS THIS ABOUT WHAT I SAID EARLIER? IF SO, I'M SORRY

I gripped my tablet with both hands, my heart dropping to the pit of my stomach.

I WON'T DO IT AGAIN

JUST PLEASE TALK TO ME

I'M WORRIED ABOUT YOU

My next breath snagged on an unwelcome sound.
Just tell him you're all right. Tell him it's not his fault. If it's really Jayde, he'll understand.
I clicked in the text box, but before I could type a character, a new message came through.

HEY, DID YOU GET THE NEW INVITE?

I mentally scrolled back through our conversation and easily deduced what that meant: Dad had been on the CB again. And I needed to know what he said.
I hesitated with my finger over the screen. What would Nic say about texting back?
If he's offering useful information, take advantage of that.

NO I DIDN'T. WHAT DID IT SAY?

The app did a somersault as it coughed up multiple messages in short succession. Aurelius sent a swear word, followed by a run-on "you're okay I was so worried." Then, as if realizing neither of those messages was a good look, he attempted to save face with:

SO YOU *HAVE* BEEN GETTING MY MESSAGES

I fought back a wave of frustration. I knew he wasn't aware of everything going on—he didn't know I'd adopted a new file I needed to keep hidden—but he should understand how much was at stake. He knew how much danger I was in, never mind my father.

THIS ISN'T ABOUT YOU. WHAT DID THE INVITE SAY?

He ignored my reproof but mercifully answered the question.

THE PARTY'S BEEN MOVED

IS IT STILL IN TOWN?

FOR NOW

I drummed my fingers on the back of the tablet to channel my nervous energy. Dad was still in town—but he was on the move, which meant that if I didn't make contact soon, I might lose him again.

HAS ANYONE I KNOW RSVP'D?

BESIDES ME? I DON'T THINK SO

So Ephesus and Cea still hadn't made contact—which meant it was up to me to catch Dad before he left town.
Aurelius had the same thought.

YOU NEED TO RSVP. NOW

He was right, but I wasn't going to do it by proxy. I needed to find a radio.
I closed the chat without responding and leapt out of bed. I threw myself into some semblance of order and tumbled down the stairs, halting just outside the kitchen door. Mr. and Mrs. Von were sitting at the island, chatting in tune to the morning news

that was broadcasting from the TV on the counter. I swallowed a prayer and braced myself for the anxiety of being reintroduced.

Be consistent, Nic had instructed. *They do have some short-term memory, but space is limited. The more consistent you are, the more likely they are to develop a pattern.*

I put on a smile and walked in like I belonged there. "Good morning, Mr. and Mrs. Von."

They both stopped midsentence and turned to stare at me.

"It's me, Andromeda, Nic's friend?" I offered.

Mrs. Von's eye twitched. "Oh, you're still here," she said finally. I passed it off with a fake laugh.

Mr. Von considered me for only a fraction of a second before he decided he still liked me. "Well, good morning! You're just in time for breakfast. Roseanne made my favorite." He finished his cup of coffee and stood to refill it.

"All food is your favorite." Mrs. Von indulged in an eyeroll that was clearly directed for me to see, and I wondered if she hated me slightly less than she did the night before. I pulled another stool up to the counter and sat down.

"Do you want some coffee…?" Mr. Von glanced back at me and squinted.

"Andromeda," I repeated.

The light returned to his eyes. "Ahh, right. How do you take it?" He grabbed another mug from the rack and started filling it before I even answered.

I hesitated. *What options are there?* "Uhh, black," I blurted, only because that's how Nic took his, and it was all I could think of.

He filled the mug nearly to the brim and slid it across the counter towards me. I accepted it and took a cautious sip. The strong, bitter flavor hit me in the teeth almost as hard as the scalding heat did. But I didn't want to look like an idiot, so I swallowed the mouthful with a smile and took another drink.

"Well, I've got to get to work. See you lovely ladies for dinner." Mr. Von grabbed a jacket from the rack and marched out of the room.

"You're retired," Mrs. Von called after him without turning around.

Mr. Von barely missed a beat. "Then I shall work on finishing this show!" He continued his stride into the living room as if that was where he had intended to go all along.

Mrs. Von turned the stove off. "Bacon or sausage, Miss...?"

"Andromeda, and bacon, please."

She nodded and, after opening and closing three separate cabinets, found a plate. She filled it with two eggs and a link of sausage and set it in front of me.

I ate the greasy meat without complaint, gears turning. If Mrs. Von couldn't remember what I'd said sixty seconds ago, she probably wouldn't remember if I asked her about an illegal radio.

"Do you know where I could get a radio?" I asked.

She gave me another whip-like stare, and I wondered if my question hadn't come off as casually as I'd intended it. "You kids still listen to the radio?" she scoffed.

I relaxed a bit. "No, no, I need it for a... school project." I took another brave sip of coffee.

She accepted the excuse with a snort. "Well, good luck with that—the last time I saw a radio was in a 2000s truck. Maybe try the junkyard."

It wasn't a terrible idea—but a young girl walking up to a junkyard asking to buy an illegal part off an old truck would probably push the bounds of suspicion. "I kind of need one that works. Any other ideas—"

I looked up and realized she wasn't listening to me at all. She stood there, deep in thought, grease dripping off her spatula.

I reached for a napkin. "Mrs. Von—?"

"Now where would he have put it?"

"Put what?"

She slapped her spatula on the counter. "Paul!" she shouted into the other room. "Didn't you used to have a radio?"

My heart restarted, and I strained to hear his answer.

"A what now?" he hollered back.

"A radio! You know, one of those walkie-talkie things. Right?" She glanced at me, looking for confirmation. I nodded encouragingly.

"I haven't seen a radio in years! Whatcha need one of those for?"

Neither of us bothered to answer him. Mrs. Von turned back to me with a shrug. "Maybe look it up online?"

That was also out of the question, but the gears were turning. Of course Mr. Von wouldn't have seen a radio in years—it had been eight since his neurosurgery. But before then he'd been a rebel, according to Nic. It wasn't out of the realm of possibility that he'd used a radio back then.

But would he still have it? He'd been a high-profile criminal; no doubt his home had been searched by government agents multiple times over the years. If there was still a radio in this house, it would have to be hidden very well.

Somewhere that had not been touched in over a decade.

I shoveled my eggs into my mouth and chased them down with a gulp of coffee. "I'll come back for the dishes," I told Mrs. Von as I stood up. "There's something I need to do for school."

She mumbled an affirmative. As soon as I left the kitchen, I heard her opening the dishwasher.

I muttered another prayer for her mental health and darted up the stairs to Nic's room.

The door creaked as I opened it, a signal I was about to step back in time. The room clearly hadn't been touched since Nic left for college, which would have been prior to his parents' surgery. It was possible the room had been overlooked by the censors.

I started at the door and searched all the way around the room, but unfortunately there wasn't much to look at. The closet was empty except for a band uniform that had been discarded like a prison jumpsuit. There were a few dried-out pens rolling around in the desk drawer, and school awards lined one shelf. The rest of the surfaces were bare.

I got down on the ground to look under the bed. *Nothing*, I groaned. *Except...*

From this angle, I could see that there was a bump in the carpet where the bookcases had been.

I knelt down and traced the rectangular indents in the carpet. There were three of them; three identical narrow bookcases must have once stood side-by-side. The carpet underneath was slightly less dusty than the rest of the room, as if the bookcases had been removed several years after Nic had moved out.

And the indent in the middle was clearly not level with the others.

I dug my fingernail into the crease and hit hard wood. I scraped and picked at it, ignoring the splinters, until the carpet loosened. I got one finger underneath the edge and pried it up. With a crack and a groan like an old man being wakened from sleep, a square panel came loose from the floor.

Underneath the floorboards was a storage compartment, filled to the brim with vintage electronics.

I reached in to grab the first object—and nearly screamed when I realized it was a gun. I carefully set it to the side and removed the rest of the objects one by one.

There was a laptop, two more guns, several ancient smartphones, and, at the very bottom, a radio.

At least, I *assumed* it was a radio. I'd never seen anything like it. It was an unmarked black box, about the size of Grandpa's vintage DVD player, with a couple of dials on the front. A corded handset was clipped to the side.

I turned one of the dials, but nothing happened. Did it need to be plugged in?

I flipped it over and looked at the back. There were several cut wires sticking out of the case; maybe the thing *had* been ripped from an old truck. But someone had turned an old laptop battery into a redneck power source with wires and electrical tape. I flipped the crudely marked "on" switch and tried the dial again.

This time I was greeted with a shower of static, and the front display lit up with the number "40."

I set the device on the edge of the bed so I was eye-level with it and started playing with the buttons. The one marked "Vol" was self-explanatory, but the rest were Greek to me: "SQ," "RF Gain." "PA." I could get the number on the display to change, but all I got through the speaker were various tones of static.

I rapped the display with my finger. It couldn't be that complicated—there were only so many options—but I couldn't just look it up on the internet. Andromeda wasn't supposed to have a radio; she certainly wouldn't look up the instructions for how to run one.

I was so engrossed in my frustration that I didn't hear the approaching footsteps over the static. The door creaked, and I nearly fell backwards into the hole in the floor.

Mr. Von stood in the doorway. He tipped his head to the side and squinted at me.

I hastily stood up and brushed off my knees. "Andromeda," I offered before he could ask.

"I know that," he said, although it was hard to tell if he meant it. "But what are you doing up here?"

"I uh… said I was going to help clean so… I thought I'd dust in here." I clapped my dirty hands together for emphasis.

He chuckled disarmingly. "You are an ambitious woman. I like it." He took two steps into the room and stopped, taking a cursory glance around. The insecurity returned to his eyes. "I don't remember what we even used this room for."

I swallowed. "I don't think it's been used in a few years," I offered.

He snorted an affirmative and glanced down at the bed. "Whatcha got there?"

I hesitated. A half-hour ago he couldn't even remember that he *had* a radio; would he remember how to work it?

I picked up the device and held it out. "Do you know what this is?"

He walked over and took it from me. He turned it over in his hands—once, twice—and my hope faltered.

Then a shot of light flashed across his face. "Ahh, my old CB! I didn't know I still had this."

Apparently the United didn't either. "Do you know how to work it?"

"*Does* it still work is the question we should be asking. This thing's older than you." He winked at me.

I smiled back. "Well, so are you, but you still work."

His large laugh filled the room. "Then there's still hope for it. Let's try it."

He sat down on the edge of the bed, and I joined him. I watched as he flipped switches and adjusted dials, trying to memorize his movements. He pressed the button on the side of the handset and coughed a "check, check" into the speaker.

Then he grabbed the largest dial and started turning it slowly. The number on the display started counting up from 1, but still all I heard was static.

"Does the static mean it's broken?" I asked after he'd gotten past 10.

"No, it just means no one's talking. Be patient."

He continued to cycle channels—and just when I'd given up hope for the fifth time in so many minutes, he hit channel 19 and I heard voices.

There were a few muttered words, like we'd jumped in at the end of a conversation. Then, loud and clear, a new voice cut through the static.

"Radio check. This is Catalyst. Are you receiving?"

"Dad," I breathed, then caught myself. I looked up at Mr. Von to see if he'd heard, but he wasn't paying attention to me. He was squinting at the device, face contorted in a frown.

There was some interference, then a voice I didn't recognize answered. "Catalyst, this is Data. 10-2, standing by."

"Thanks, Data. Requesting 10-13, Brighton and Malvern. Over."

I had no idea what 10-13 meant, but Brighton was a major road less than a mile from here.

Dad's here—he's right here!

I grabbed Mr. Von's knee. "Can we talk back?"

He didn't respond. He held the device up and pressed his ear to it, even though the volume was on max.

The stranger on the other end of the line spoke again. "Does anyone have a visual on Brighton and Malvern?"

There was silence—a long silence—and I thought we'd lost them. I grabbed the handset and held it to my lips—then realized I had no idea what to say. I couldn't just announce my location and tell Dad to meet me on the street corner. But he was *right there*—I had to do something.

A third voice joined the conversation before I could decide. "Catalyst, be advised we've got bears. Over."

"What's a bear?" I wondered aloud. It had to be some kind of code—there was no way there were actual bears in downtown Allston.

"It's a cop," Mr. Von mumbled.

I stared at him. Was he remembering?

"What's 10-13 mean then?" I pressed, hoping to milk more out of his window of sanity. But he said nothing more—I don't think he realized he'd spoken at all—and continued to gaze in wonder at the device in his lap, as if he'd just given birth to it.

There was broken chatter, and then Dad clipped in again. "10-4, thanks for that."

I tried to piece the information together. Dad must have been asking if that intersection was clear to pass through— which, apparently, it wasn't.

How could I tell him I was nearby and safe?

"Catalyst, this is Data again. 10-25 Blue Fire?"

I froze. He was asking about me.

The pause before Dad responded was palpable. "Negative, Data."

My heart broke. *I'm right here, Dad!*

Data sighed into the line. "Roger that. Data over and out."

Even I knew what that meant—they were about to hang up. Who knew how long it would be before Dad would sign on again—and if he moved out of range, I'd never be able to reach him on the radio.

I can't lose him again!

I pressed down on the handheld. "Catalyst, this is Blue Fire. I'm here."

10

The silence was deafening, so much so that I thought they'd already signed off. I was about to repeat myself when multiple voices started competing at once.

"Oh my—"

"Blue Fire, this is Data, 10-20?"

"Green Dragon, are you reading this?"

"10-45, we need a fox hunt."

"Blue Fire, this is Data, do you copy?"

And through it all my father's voice cut like a knife. "Blue Fire, 10-41-32, *now.*"

I hadn't heard that tone of voice in almost ten years—not since that one time Ephesus had goaded me into sneaking into Grandpa's attic and we'd broken an irreplaceable antique. That was the tone of voice you did not disobey—except I had no idea what he was asking me to do.

I'd forgotten Mr. Von was there until he lurched, bouncing the radio on his knees. "Switch to channel 32!" he declared gleefully, and then thankfully did just that—since I was still figuring out how to change the channel.

He flipped a dial, and my father's voice came in mid-sentence. "—you copy? Blue Fire!"

"Da—I mean Catalyst, it's me, I copy," I cried into the receiver.

"What are you doing?" There was that tone of voice again. "You need to get off the radio—now."

"It's fine, I'm safe." I glanced at Mr. Von, as if to confirm my statement. He was watching me with a wild grin, as if this was the most fun he'd had in years.

"No, you're not!" Dad seemed to realize he was shouting. He lowered his voice and sped up his words. "Listen, we only have a minute before they figure out we're on this channel. Stay off the radio. Tell no one where you are. Don't trust anyone."

Use him, but don't trust him.

I swallowed back fear. "I know, but it's okay, I found a safe place. I need you to meet me here. I can get us out of this."

"It's *not* safe. I need you to lay low; they know you're in this neighborhood now. Don't log any electronic activity. They're looking for you."

I wanted to blurt the truth—that I had a clean file, and money, and I could get us back to Mars, if only we could make contact.

Dad didn't give me a chance and kept talking. "Don't use the radio—they can track you as long as you're transmitting. I'll call you on Tuesday, at 20:30, channel 2."

Tuesday? That was a whole three days from now. I opened my mouth to object—but the Holy Spirit washed over me with all the truths I couldn't deny.

You can trust him.

You can trust Me.

"10-4, Catalyst," I said with a peace I did not feel.

He sighed, and for a second there was a crack in his armor. "I love you, Blue Fire. I'm so sorry—"

Other voices cut into the line and talked over him.

"Blue Fire, do you read?"

"Catalyst, hold your position."

"10-45, anyone tracking?"

I barely caught Dad's "over and out" through the clamor. I hung there, listening to their frantic chatter, fighting competing waves of loneliness and joy. Then I reached down to turn the device off, silencing the noise.

Mr. Von sat there for another minute, still grinning wildly, as if he expected there to be more. When nothing happened, he seemed to come back down to Earth, and whatever buoyancy had been sustaining his sanity faded. The dull and distracted look returned to his eyes, and he offered me a weak smile.

"Well, that was fun. Thanks for letting me play." He stood up and handed the radio to me.

I took it. "Sure. Thanks for the help." I set the device, which suddenly felt light and cheap, in my lap. The handset slid off and dangled by its coiled cord.

He gave my shoulder a squeeze and left.

I watched the handset bounce until the motion stilled. *Tuesday?* I wouldn't hear from Dad again until Tuesday night, and what was I supposed to do until then? I had to stay off the radio, and Andromeda couldn't do anything suspicious online. I probably shouldn't even go outside.

Apparently the best thing I could do was absolutely nothing, and that felt utterly wrong.

I picked up the handset and clipped it on the radio. Dad said he would call me Tuesday—which meant he would still be in the area. He wouldn't do anything without me, not this time.

I knelt down and put the rest of the gadgets back under the floor. I picked up one of the old smartphones and turned it over in my hand. Cea had used a phone just like it when she called for help. After some thought, I set the phone aside, then put everything else away and replaced the panel.

I took the cellphone and radio and hid them under the far corner of Cea's bed, in a box of off-season clothes. I didn't figure the Vons got many visitors, but the last thing I needed was someone walking in and seeing the radio on the counter.

As soon as that task was finished, anxiety and restlessness tried to shove their way back into my vacated brain. I knew I had to keep myself busy, so I decided to do what I'd promised: Clean.

After asking Mrs. Von where her cleaning supplies were (and then spending ten minutes finding them myself because the closet she indicated wasn't the correct one), I started in Nic's room. I'd disturbed enough of the dust crawling around on the floor that my footprints in the carpet led like a treasure map right to the hidden panel. I dusted the room top-down, shook out the comforter, and vacuumed three times in an attempt to restore the carpet to its original shade. The bookcase-size dents in the floor still seemed obvious to me, so with some effort I managed to drag the drafting board across the room and cover up the panel.

By then it was lunchtime, during which Mr. Von subjected me to another cup of coffee because apparently he was ready for his third (or fourth). This time I had no excuse not to stay at the table and eat slowly like a well-adjusted person, so I forced myself to finish the whole cup.

I took over dish-duty and then decided to continue the trend and clean the whole kitchen. Mrs. Von had done her best to keep up with it, but the inside of the fridge was a nightmare. It was clear grocery shopping was a struggle for her. She had six or more packages of all the common ingredients. Most of them were dated only days apart, as if she bought a new one every time she went shopping. There were numerous expired items, some of which had grown into a biohazard. It took me several hours to get it back in order and wipe down all the shelves.

After that I needed a bath. Nic had, as usual, undersold the faultiness of the upstairs shower; I was practically done before the water was anything more than tepid. But then again, it took me half as long to wash my hair now that it was so short.

I came back to my room just in time to hear my tablet vomit up several notifications. I skimmed the lockscreen and was unsurprised to find a tirade from Aurelius. He had evidently heard about my brief radio appearance and was less than pleased that I'd come back to Earth without telling him.

I skimmed the messages, several of which were punctuated with foul words, until I got to the bottom.

LOOK, I KNOW YOU'RE HOME FROM COLLEGE. YOU CAN COME TO THE PARTY. WHY WON'T YOU LET ME PICK YOU UP?

THERE'S A MALL NEAR YOUR PLACE. WHY DON'T WE MEET THERE TOMORROW? I'LL BUY YOU LUNCH

I cringed. There was, in fact, a mall near here—which he would know because I'd given away my general area by being on the CB.

It was unavoidable that he knew I was in town, but I didn't like the fact that he was watching my every move, trying to deduce my whereabouts like I was a math problem to be solved. Couldn't he take no for an answer?

Maybe Nic had been right about him all along.

I muted Aurelius for twenty-four hours and closed the app.

By the time I got back downstairs, Mrs. Von was cooking again. Just like Nic had predicted, she seemed less startled to see me each subsequent time I walked in the room, as if the repetition were softening her nerves. She actually let me help with dinner, and I was able to keep us on track and follow the recipe through to completion. Mr. Von was delighted with the results.

Mrs. Von wouldn't let me clean up; she'd said I'd "done enough," which made me wonder if she'd noticed the inside of her fridge and managed to put two and two together. I tried to excuse myself, but Mr. Von haggled me into the living room to watch a sitcom. It was censored media, which meant it was lifeless and boring and agonizingly politically correct, but I enjoyed watching him guffaw after every punchline.

Sunday and Monday went much the same, with Mr. Von giving me way too much coffee (he didn't even ask this time) and

Mrs. Von making a concentrated effort not to hate me. I cleaned the living room, dining room, Cea's room, and the upstairs bathroom. Mrs. Von wouldn't let me anywhere near their master, but I hoped she would change her mind after she saw how beautiful the rest of the house looked. I was running out of places to clean.

Monday night, I voluntarily followed Mr. Von into the living room after dinner. Mrs. Von joined us and read on her tablet. We spent the evening in companionable silence, with me wondering if this was what Nic's childhood had been like.

Surely there was a point in time when Mr. Von wouldn't have been content to sit in front of a TV all day. You didn't put humans on Mars by being idle. How much of this man's personality had been artificially manufactured by the neurosurgery? What had he been like before then? Could that man be ever brought back?

I turned on my tablet and started researching neurosurgery. I figured no one would question my internet history when my file clearly stated I was staying with people who had undergone the procedure.

The theory behind the pseudoscience was simple: If a person was noncompliant, perhaps they could be rewired to fit the mold. After all, according to the government, all the troublesome things that made us individuals—religion, nationality, race— were figments of our imagination, fictitious constructs we created around flawed thinking. To them, the human brain was little more than a stubborn computer, and computers could be reprogrammed.

Unlike the failed brainwashing attempts of the 2060s, neurosurgery didn't "erase" memories. Instead, it rewired the neural pathways to avoid problematic triggers. The theory was that if you could block out a person's emotional reaction to words like "God" and "Bible," they'd cease to be Christian, or at least stop behaving like one.

The problem was that test subjects also stopped doing a lot of other things—including, in some cases, breathing. Everyone who had undergone the procedure ended up like the Vons or worse. Apparently you couldn't just cut people's identity out of their brains like ripping a page from a book.

But if the surgery didn't touch long-term memory, that meant the memories were still in there, weren't they? Could those neural pathways be reconnected? If a brain could be reprogrammed once, surely it could be reprogrammed again.

A quick internet search revealed that other people had been asking the same questions. As of yet, experimental therapy had been unsuccessful—but at least they were trying.

Unlike Nic.

I was deeply engrossed in some stupidly-hard-to-interpret medical journal when someone jangled a key in the back door.

I froze and told my irritable pulse that I'd heard wrong. But then I heard the door open and the screen door slam shut, and I jumped up.

Mr. and Mrs. Von either hadn't heard or weren't concerned, because they both just gazed at me curiously.

"Someone's here," I hissed.

Mr. Von shrugged. "Probably grocery delivery."

"It's nine o'clock at night!" I returned, and realized I sounded exactly like Mrs. Von.

I briefly considered running. I didn't know who could be visiting the Vons—after dark, and coming through the back door—but whoever it was, they didn't need to know I was here. But the only place to go was the kitchen, and light footsteps were already coming down the hall.

Both Mr. and Mrs. Von stood up as a woman strode into the living room. She threw the hood of her dark jacket back, revealing a halo of tangled blonde curls.

"Mom and Dad, I'm home."

11

“Cea!”

She looked as surprised as I was to see a visitor in her parents’ living room. She flipped her jacket back and put her hand on the gun she was not-so-subtly carrying in her pocket.

“Who are you?” she demanded. She took in my bleached hair and angsty outfit and, apparently, didn’t recognize me at first glance. I would have been flattered if I didn’t think I was about to get shot.

“It’s me.” I put my hands up and spoke slowly so she could hear my voice.

She took me in again, and her eyes lit up. “Philadelphia!” she cried, a burst of raw emotion garbling the word. She ran at me and engulfed me in a hug.

“Who are you?” Mrs. Von demanded, at the same time her husband said, “Who’s Philadelphia? I thought your name was…”

“Andromeda,” I said, giving Cea’s shoulder a warning squeeze.

She separated herself from me. “Right, Andromeda, sorry.” She took a sharp breath to compose herself and turned to her parents with a plastic smile. "Hi, Mom and Dad, it's me—Cea—remember?"

When it was clear they didn't, I stepped in. "Remember that doctor I told you about? Nic? He's her brother."

All three of them repeated Nic's name with various inflections. Mr. Von acted like this was the first he'd heard of the man—Mrs. Von looked like she might remember, but that only made her more suspicious—and Cea went unhinged.

"Nic! He's okay? Have you seen him?"

I silenced her with a warning glance.

"This man sure gets around," Mrs. Von muttered, then shifted her scrutiny back to Cea. "How'd you get in?"

"You gave me a key, remember?" Cea held up the tiny silver object.

Mrs. Von frowned at it but couldn't deny its existence, so she shifted gears. "And what are you doing here?"

Cea sighed and pocketed the key. "I came back for a visit."

"I'm sensing a trend here." Mrs. Von glanced at her husband, but to no avail. He'd already settled back in his armchair.

"If she's a friend of Nic's, she's welcome here! Andi, show her upstairs, why don't you."

"Of course." I grabbed my tablet and led the way up the stairs before Mrs. Von could attempt any more negotiations.

As soon as the bedroom door shut behind us, Cea started gushing again. "Phil! I can't believe you're all right. How did you get here?"

"Nic sent me." I gestured at the bed, hoping she'd sit down and remember to breathe.

"Nic *sent* you? Where is he? Is he all right? Does he—"

I put my hand up to stop her. "Why don't you let me explain from the beginning?"

She let out the breath she apparently forgot she was holding. "Sorry. You're right. It's just... been a week." She shed her coat and sat down on the bed, then looked around the room. "What are you doing in my room? Couldn't you have picked Nic's?"

"I liked your style of decorating better," I laughed, even though that wasn't exactly the truth.

She smiled as I sat down next to her. She wrapped me in another hug—softer and longer this time. After a minute, she sat back and studied me.

"You look different. I like your earrings."

"Different was the intent." I studied her in return. She looked like she was in one piece, but the blood and dirt under her broken fingernails told a different story. "What happened to you?"

She gave a morbid chuckle. "Going to make me go first, eh? What have you heard?"

I paused to take my tablet offline, just in case. "Only what Thames told me. He said you escaped, but I never knew how much of that was the truth."

She nodded. "It happened pretty much like you think it did. The virus—that was you, wasn't it?"

"More Nic than me, but yeah."

She smiled, the implications not lost on her. "They had me in solitary. The virus made a mess of the security systems and had all the guards running around like chickens with their heads cut off—it wasn't that hard to slip out."

I sent up a prayer of thanks. "So where have you been?"

"I went off the grid. I wanted to see how things would blow over—and then I heard about your videos. I was sure Nic and I were going to get flagged in the investigation—but we never did. Then suddenly Thames was dead, and I realized no one was looking for me. So I decided to come here."

"Why didn't you call Nic?" I asked.

She shot me a look. "First of all, I didn't know he was back on Mars. Second of all, my file still says I live in a containment camp. If I logged any electronic activity, they would have arrested me and thrown me back in prison."

I flinched. "So that's why you've been offline."

She groaned and popped her neck. "You have no idea how freaking long it takes to walk across this city."

"I'm so glad you're safe." I indulged in a laugh, but the sound died halfway through when I remembered someone else. I sat up and grabbed her arm. "Have you heard from Ephesus?"

"No," she said quietly, as if she were afraid to let me down. She looked at her hands and traced the scratches on her knuckles. "Your dad was being held somewhere else, and Ephesus was still in the hospital—or so they said."

My heart fluttered weakly. "Was he—"

"He's alive," she corrected. "They said he had a few broken bones and a smashed nose, but nothing internal. I'm sure he's fine now." She reached up and squeezed my hand.

I tried to console us both with a smile. "He must have escaped, or we'd have heard about it. His file says he's still missing."

She nodded but did not return the smile. "And your dad?"

I straightened. "I just heard from him. He got on the CB a few days ago—that's why I'm here."

"The CB?" she said, in exactly the same tone I'd used when I first heard it. "That means he's still in Boston?" Without waiting for an answer to that question, she spilled several more. "And how did *you* get here? Where was he keeping you? Your file is a mess, girl. You can't even sneeze in public without getting the cops called on you. How did you—"

"Whoa, maybe it's my turn to explain." She conceded with a nod, so I continued. "I have a new file."

"So that's Andromeda?"

"Yeah, Andromeda Nolan." I let the name hang in the air.

She jerked. "Nolan? You're kidding, right?"

"I wish."

"Well, this will be a good story." She yanked her muddy boots off, fluffed the pillows up against the headboard, and settled back. "I'm listening."

I folded my legs under me and told her everything that had happened since we'd been separated—including how I'd come to acquire my enemy's last name.

"That explains why Mrs. Nolan was so nice to you, and why Thames let her get away with so much," Cea mused.

"Unfortunately," I muttered, trying to keep the bitterness out of my voice.

"Guess we owe her a thank you." Cea tipped her head. "Do you know what happened to her?"

"Hopefully she ran when the government busted Thames's office," I said, avoiding her eyes. I really did hope the woman had escaped—I had no desire for her to be hanged for her husband's crimes—but I also didn't want to see her again. I hoped wherever she went had taken her far away from me.

"She visited me a couple times before I broke out." Cea detangled her curls with her fingers. "Gave me updates on Ephesus."

I nodded and hoped that was the end of the conversation.

"So Nic..." Cea sat up straight. "...is governor again? He's still on Mars? Can you get ahold of him?"

"Yes, yes, and yes." I grabbed my tablet and brought it back online. "Carnegie kept the base clean—the United has no idea anything happened on Mars. Nic was able to basically pick up where he left off—minus the plot to start World War IV with acid rain."

A dry smile tugged at her lips. "Let's hope so."

I opened the messaging app. There was a fresh batch of notifications from Aurelius, but I ignored them and started an audio call with Nic.

It rang through the first time. I glanced at the dark sky outside the window and wondered what time it was over there. Not that it mattered; I'm sure even if it was 3am he would be glad he took this call.

I dialed him again. This time he answered after one ring. "This better be important, Andromeda." He sounded fully awake, and I heard other people talking in the background. "Because there's a lot of money hinging on this meeting."

"Of course it's important." I enabled video and angled the camera to face Cea.

"Nic," she called.

He swore. There was clattering and hurried apologies to the others in the room, then footsteps. A door slammed, and his camera blinked on.

"Laodicea." His voice was soft, but his face was hard as he searched her, as if making sure it was really her.

"Nic," she repeated. She took the tablet from me and held it up to her face. "You're okay."

"Never better. Where are you?"

"Mom's house. I realized the United wasn't after me or you, so I made my way here."

"Watch what you say," he reminded her coldly. "But I'm glad you're safe. Now come home."

The abrupt suggestion killed Cea's smile. "I'm sorry, what?"

"Come home," he repeated in exactly the same tone as before.

"You want me to jump on a transit and come back to base?"

"Unless they've invented another way to get to Mars, that's what I'd recommend."

She rubbed her forehead with one hand. "Nic, I can't just 'come home.'"

"Why not?" he responded, which was exactly what I was wondering.

"My file still says I live—"

"A clerical error. You've signed the file, have you not?"

"I mean yeah, but the transit ticket—"

"I'll buy it," I offered.

Nic cleared his throat. "I'm not *that* poor, Andi." I couldn't see the screen from where I was, but I could perfectly imagine what expression went with that attitude.

"No, you don't get it. I can't come back yet, Nic. I've got to find Eph—"

"He's a grown man, last I checked. Let him find himself."

I flinched. He wasn't wrong—he rarely was, it seemed—but I would have said it with a lot more grace. I tried to translate. "Nic's right. Let him come to you. He'd want to know you're safe."

Cea looked up at me. "Yeah? And what are *you* doing here?"

I opened my mouth, then realized I had no good answer to that. *Exactly what I just told you not to do...*

"Andromeda has her own affairs to attend to," Nic said. "Yours are up here. Come home."

Cea wagged her head. "No. I'm not leaving until everyone is safe."

"Then you'll be waiting a very long time, which is exactly why we're not going to have this conversation."

She glared at the screen. "You're right, because I've made my decision."

"Cea."

"Nic, I'm serious."

"Cea," he repeated, harder and slower.

"I'm not coming home, Nic."

He sighed. "Don't make me do it."

I could have sworn Cea turned white, but she held her ground. "Do what, Nic? What are you going to do?"

He prefaced with some expletives. "You're *really* going to make me do this, aren't you?"

"Do, uh, I need to leave?" I offered.

They both ignored me. "I'm not *making* you do anything, Nic. You're the one being a jerk."

"Fine! Fine, fine, fine, fine..." His voice faded and returned, as if he'd gotten up to take a lap around the desk. "You want me to be the bad guy? I'll be the bad guy."

I swallowed. Being the villain hadn't gone well for him last time—and I could tell it was about to go very poorly now.

"Laodicea," he said, using the name like a threat.

She gave him one last warning. "Don't."

"I'm *ordering* you to come home."

Now it was Cea's turn to growl, drop the tablet, and storm around the room. "You can't tell me what to do!" she screeched.

"Actually, as the commanding governor of the base you're supposed to be stationed on, I can."

I cringed as Cea's face flushed redder than the surface of Mars itself. "You know I *hate* it when you do that."

"I honestly don't care what you think right now," he returned, although I had long since figured that out for myself.

Cea spun back around and gestured emphatically at the tablet, even though she was nowhere in view of the camera. "And what about Phil, huh?"

"Andi," both Nic and I said at the same time.

"You want me to just leave her here alone?"

"Please don't bring me into this..." I said, entirely to myself.

Nic shrugged. "She got there just fine on her own."

"She's a child, Nic!"

"Excuse me?" I grunted.

"In more ways than one," Nic agreed. "But unlike you, I can't tell her what to do."

The delicious irony of that statement was too great to resist. "Uh, actually, you can," I said, fully realizing I wasn't helping.

"Andromeda, don't you dare—"

Cea shot me a look.

"Technically, he's my legal guardian right now."

Nic muttered something foul under his breath.

Cea stood frozen in the middle of the room for a beat. She looked at me, then back at the tablet. "Well, nice to see you two have kissed and made up."

"Yes," Nic regained his composure, "and our newfound friendship is going to be the death of me. I would be happy to tell you all about it if you would *just come home!*"

At that moment, our bedroom door creaked open. "Girls? What's all this shouting? Are you all right?" Mrs. Von stepped into the room, backlit by the much brighter light in the hallway.

Cea waved her off. "It's nothing, we're just talking..."

"Hi Mom," Nic chirped from the tablet.

Mrs. Von cocked her head. "Who's that?" She walked over to the bed.

My heart lurched. "Remember that doctor I was telling you about? The one who took me in after my parents died?" I snatched the tablet and held it up for her to see. "This is him. This is Nic."

She leaned over and squinted at his image.

Nic stared back calmly, letting her study him. "How is Paul?"

She seemed tickled that he asked. "Oh, he's good. You knew him, right?"

I jumped. Did she remember our earlier conversation? I cast an eager glance at Cea, but she was just watching her mom blankly, eyes dry and glazed.

"Very well," Nic responded. "He's a brilliant man."

Mrs. Von straightened. "That was a nice thing you did for Andromeda, taking her in. She's a good girl."

"Despite her best efforts," Nic agreed. I blushed.

Mrs. Von smiled. "I bet your parents are very proud of you for taking care of her like that."

Cea sucked in a crippled breath. I searched Mrs. Von's face, looking for any emotion, any recognition of what she was saying.

Nic was slow to respond, but when he did, his voice was filled with more confidence than I expected. "I know they are."

"Well." Mrs. Von walked away. "You girls try to keep it down. Paul's asleep in his armchair like he always is. And don't stay up too late—it's a school night."

"Yes ma'am," I called as she closed the door behind herself.

I turned back to Cea. Her face was unreadable, but the interaction seemed to have taken the fight out of her—which for the moment was probably a good thing. She sat back down on the bed.

"Come home, Cea," Nic said again, this time at least making an attempt to be polite.

She sighed. "I just don't feel good about leaving Ph—Andromeda here alone. She's a teenager, Nic, and she's looking for the most wanted man on the eastern seaboard. You want me to just leave her out here to find her dad by herself? She could get killed, Nic."

I couldn't tell by her expression whether she was actually afraid for my life or just using me as bait. She was obviously scared—but of what?

Nic remained calm. "I am fully aware of the immense risk she's putting herself in. Unfortunately, the last time I tried to keep her here against her will, she blew up a lab, depressurized an entire wing, and I spent six months in jail. Hence, I am reserving that as a last resort."

I chuckled dryly, but Nic cut me off mid-laugh. "That said, if you pull another stunt like you did Saturday, Andi, I *swear* I will send Sardis down to get you."

Cea arched an eyebrow at me. I felt my neck grow hot as two revelations—both of which should have been obvious from the start—suddenly dawned on me.

Nic hadn't wanted me to go.

And he was keeping an eye on me from afar.

"Yessir," I mumbled, somewhat culled.

"Well, what do you think happens if you keep *me* up there against my will?" Cea inserted herself back into the conversation.

"Same thing that always happens," Nic said without hesitation. "You don't talk to me for three weeks."

Cea huffed, and suddenly their relationship made a whole lot more sense.

"But I think I can live with that if I know you're safe."

She was silent.

Nic sighed. "Look, I'm aware Andromeda has put herself—and, quite frankly, the rest of us—in a dangerous position. But that was her choice."

I tensed. His statement lingered in my soul and stirred an emotion I couldn't quite identify.

"But I can—" Cea started.

"I can't begrudge her for taking care of her family," Nic interrupted. "But I need to take care of mine."

She finally looked into the camera again.

"Come home, Cea. Please."

She didn't say anything for a long moment. Then, finally, she nodded.

He released the emotional tension with a sigh. "Thank you. Text me once you have your itinerary."

She nodded again, then stood up and walked across the room. I picked the tablet up.

"Andromeda."

I looked down at the screen to find him staring at me, hard.

"Remember what I said."

"Yessir," I said again, and he hung up.

12

I set the tablet down and waited for Cea to speak first.

She spent a long minute staring at one of the many rock band posters plastered on her wall. "I need a shower," she declared finally. She grabbed some of her old clothes from the closet and stormed out of the room.

My tablet dinged with a message from Nic. He said Cea's file had been corrected and asked if I could please book her transit ticket right away. He added that he would pay me back.

I acknowledged the message and pulled up the travel site Mr. Sardis had shown me. The earliest flight was for Thursday afternoon. The price was significantly higher than what I had paid a mere week before—she could save several thousand if she waited a few more days—but I went ahead and bought the ticket. I took a grand off the amount I told Nic and hoped he wouldn't question it.

Cea returned shortly after, her hair hanging in wet waves around her face. She flopped backwards on the bed with a grunt.

"I hate him," she announced.

"Don't we all. You're leaving Wednesday." I put my tablet on the charger.

"I'm kicking you out of my room tonight." She rolled over on her side and looked at me. "So what's your plan, exactly? You said your dad's on the CB? How'd you find this out?"

For an answer, I got down on my knees and pulled the box of sweaters out from under the bed. I tossed the radio and the old smartphone on the comforter.

She sat up. "Where did you get these?"

"They were hiding in the floor in your brother's room."

"So that's where Dad hid his gear." She flipped the phone over in her hand. "Were there more phones?"

"Yeah, a couple."

"Good, I'm going to show you how to set up a burner phone." She powered the device on. "Old smartphones make the best burners because of one key feature—emergency calling."

The lock screen brightened. She held the home button until the "Emergency Call" text appeared. "It's the law that every phone has to be able to dial 911, even if the user is out of cell service or data or whatever."

"So? Even my tablet can do that." I picked up my device and pressed the "emergency" icon on the home screen. The screen flashed white and asked me if I wanted to contact emergency services.

Text in the corner caught my eye: *Emergency Contact.* I clicked on it.

Nic's profile appeared. I smiled.

Cea didn't notice. "Yeah, but United cell service is free, so it's kind of a moot point. Newer devices just treat it like any other call. The old phones basically bypass all verifications and connect to whatever signal they can find when you activate emergency mode. That means, with a bit of messing around in the settings, you can get it to make calls *without* registering the device on the database."

I made a noise of admiration.

"Trouble is, when an unregistered device like a cellphone connects to the network, it raises massive red flags in the algorithm. They're almost always going to investigate it—which means they'll see what phone number you're using, who you called, what you said, and, if you keep using the same device, probably track the signal."

"So use it to order pizza and then ditch it," I concluded.

"Exactly." She opened the menu and showed me how to change the settings. I made her repeat the steps twice so I could memorize them. Then she powered off the device and pocketed it. "Now I need a real phone. If I'm going to fly to Mars, they're going to expect me to be online."

"I can buy you one tomorrow. Do you want some better clothes, too?" I eyed the garishly juvenile outfit she'd chosen.

"Sure, let's have a girl's day out, why not. Here, you should take this." She got up to root around in the dirty clothes she'd tossed on the floor. She found her parents' house key and pressed it into my palm.

"Why do I need this?"

"So you can get in when they're not home—and without leaving an electronic log." She sat back down on the bed. "Nic took the keypad on the back door offline years ago so we could keep using the manual lock. If you go through the front or garage door, there will be an electronic log associated with your fingerprints. Of course, if you want to stay completely offline, you also don't want to connect to the home internet with any registered devices."

I nodded. I grabbed my backpack and hid the key in an inner pocket where it wouldn't get lost.

Cea picked up the radio. "This thing still works?"

"Surprisingly. Do you remember your dad using it?"

"A little." A tangle of vague emotions clouded her voice. "I wasn't around for most of my parents' rebellious phase. As soon as things started getting serious—and Dad started getting in real trouble with the law—Nic petitioned child services to put me in boarding school. He took custody of me as soon as he became governor. The government, of course, was happy to hand me over."

I couldn't decide whether that was endearing or horrifying—or a sinister combination of both—so I stayed silent.

She ran her hand over the device. "I guess that's one thing we have in common now—Nic's decided it's his job to take care of us."

I snorted doubtfully. "I'm sure as soon as my dad's back online Nic will be more than happy to give me up."

"About that." Cea set the radio aside. "Your file must have cost millions to forge—there's no way you can concoct the same thing for your father *and* Ephesus, at least not on short notice. What's your plan, girl?"

"I just have to get them back to Mars," I said with resounding confidence, hoping the strength in my voice would convince both me and her. "Nic says it's not hard to forge a temp file. It might not look legitimate under scrutiny, but if it'll buy a transit ticket, it'll do. Nic already agreed they can come live on base."

A genuine smile briefly brightened Cea's features before vanishing back into obscurity. "Do you have someone who can forge a temp file?"

I rooted around in my backpack until I found the business card Nic had given me. I held it out to her. "I'm supposed to tell him Nic sent me."

She took the paper and squinted at it. Her eyes lit up, and she turned back to me with a grin. "Want to get a tattoo?"

13

If I thought the tattoo parlors on Mars were sketchy, the ones in the inner city of Boston were even worse.

It was the next day, and Cea and I had ventured downtown. Our first stop had been a gas station across the street from her parents' house, where Cea traded a scan of her fingerprints for a bus pass. I was impressed those still existed, but Cea explained that they were exactly for situations like this. If a citizen lost their electronic devices—or couldn't afford any—the United still wanted to track their movements. Most people were happy to trade security for a free ride.

We took the bus to a shopping center, where I bought Cea a new cellphone. The bored sales rep made her register it on the database before he removed the security tag.

After that, we took the bus to a different shopping center across town to buy clothes. We bounced from mall to mall until we had everything Cea needed, avoiding staying in one place for long. I was a wanted woman, after all.

I'd spent the first hour of our trip guiltily scanning the crowd, foolishly hoping I'd see Dad or Ephesus and desperately hoping I wouldn't see Jayde. But of course I didn't see anyone I knew—and no one else seemed to recognize me either. No one gave me a second glance, not even the store clerks who looked me right in the eye. Apparently my dark eyeliner, ripped jeans, and ashy hair had me blending in with the mall crowd perfectly.

I was just beginning to relax when Cea took us to a part of town I definitely knew we shouldn't be in.

The street reeked of decay. The buildings seemed to draw in on themselves, leering over the broken sidewalk as if they were trying to block out the sun. Trash clogged the gutter, and the sewer smelled rancid. And the men at the bus stop definitely stared—although not, I'm sure, because I reminded them of Philadelphia Smyrna.

"You sure about that tattoo?" Cea grinned at me as she continued walking, as if the decrepit atmosphere had no effect on her.

"No—I mean yes." I yanked my eyes away from the street and tried to pull myself together. "No tattoos. Final answer."

I followed her into an alley. The row was lined with several shops—none of which looked like places I should be patronizing.

"Suit yourself. I have a fun one on my shoulder blade."

"You do?"

She winked at me. "Don't tell Nic."

She led me to the shop at the end of the alley. The tinted windows were marked with same mountain range that was on the business card. Cea shoved the door open, and I followed, muttering a prayer for protection under my breath.

The interior was somehow both dank and neon-lit at the same time. It was definitely a tattoo and piercing parlor—not unlike the one I visited on Mars—although judging by the various advertisements on the wall, they also did other augmentations as well. One sign even suggested they offered experimental brain implants. Mercifully, the shop was vacant.

A stocky man in a kilt emerged from the back. I couldn't help but stare—it had been at least a decade since I'd seen anyone wear a kilt in public. Regional costume wasn't technically illegal, but it was a good way to get yourself reported for a hate crime—even if you were a native.

"Like it, lass?" he said, laying the accent on thick for my benefit. He was muscular, with a fierce short beard and a proud manbun. Most of his visible skin was decorated with a kaleidoscope of Celtic knots, dragons, and ancient symbols of horses, men, and eagles.

"Progressive," I said, and he winked.

"Andes." Cea's voice dripped with enough butter to bake a potato. She sidled up to the counter and leaned on it. "Remember me?"

He squinted at her, eyes nearly disappearing behind his chiseled cheekbones. "Got any of my work on ya?"

She rolled up her sleeve until she revealed a tiny symbol on the inside of her upper arm—somewhere almost no one would have seen. It looked like a bird with a lightning bolt, but she pushed her sleeve back down before I could get a better look.

Andes broke into a grin. "Well, if it isn't my favorite wayward girl, Laodicea. Your brother ain't anywhere around, is he? You know how he feels about you getting work done."

"Actually, he sent us."

The atmosphere in the room changed immediately. Andes's smile faded. "The great Dr. Von referred me? I don't believe that for a minute," he said, although the clipped tone of his voice implied the opposite.

Cea nodded at me. I reached into my backpack, withdrew the business card, and threw it on the counter.

Andes glared at it but didn't pick it up. His jaw tensed, causing the tattoos on his neck to ripple. "And what if I say I'm not in business anymore?"

Cea sighed. "Andes, please, this is import—"

I put my hand up to stop her. I found the man's gaze and held it. "I'll pay in advance."

He barked a laugh. "You?"

I pulled out my tablet, opened the payment app, and handed the device to him. "Name your price."

His wolfish smile returned, and some air came back into the room. "You sure do know the way to a man's heart, lass."

He reached below the counter and pulled out a thick rubber mat. He unrolled it and laid my tablet on it. "Phone, please," he grunted at Cea.

She nodded and tossed her device on the mat. At my quizzical stare, Andes explained, "Dampening field. I don't take chances." He pulled his phone from his pocket and added it to the pile.

"And neither do we," Cea resumed control of the conversation. "We need two temp files and fingerprint alterations to go with them."

"Two? Are these credentials for you lovely ladies?"

Cea snorted derisively. "Our affairs are in order, thank you."

"I'm sure they are. How long do these files need to last?"

"Long enough to buy a transit ticket," I answered, and hoped that wasn't revealing too much.

"To where?"

"Nowhere you're going."

He ran a tongue over his teeth. "And when do you need this done by?"

I looked to Cea. "We'll let you know when we're ready," she replied with a toss of her curls.

"Say no more," Andes chuckled, which was good, because I wasn't comfortable giving him any more information. He reached under the counter again and pulled out a vintage paper logbook. It was filled with names and data from some business that had probably died before computers were born.

Andes flipped to a page in the middle and stabbed his finger at a random entry. He glanced up at me. "Guy name, gal name, or don't care?"

"Male names, please." It didn't matter a whole lot, but Ephesus would have a very hard time convincing anyone that his real name was even remotely feminine.

"How about... Michael Eddington for lucky guy number one, and..." Andes slid a pencil out of the spiral of the logbook and added a number next to the entry he'd picked. Then he flipped to a new page and selected another random name. "Reginald Barclay for wingman number two."

"Sure," I said dismissively, as if I had any idea what a convincing fake name sounded like. I hadn't exactly had a hand in inventing my own.

Andes picked up the business card and copied the numbers from the logbook onto the back. "When you're ready, tell the boys to call Andes and say they have an appointment with these confirmation codes. I'll take care of the rest."

He slid the card across the counter. I pinned it with my finger. The process sounded simple enough—except for the fact that I would probably have to give my father and brother this information over the radio. "And what if someone were to overhear me telling them to 'call Andes'?"

He was prepared for the question. "Andes isn't my real name, and this number isn't traceable—at least not to anywhere on this continent."

"And what if another one of your clients happens to be eavesdropping? I can't be the only girl so lucky as to secure your services."

"My clients know better than to interrupt a deal. Not when I know who they used to be." His eyes glittered wickedly, as if he would relish the chance to make someone pay.

"Duly noted." I picked up the card and returned it to the inner pocket of my backpack. "Thank you."

"No, thank *you.*" He picked up his phone and started typing. "Let me draw up the contract for your surgery so you can sign off on it, and we'll get you paid up."

"My *what?*" I said, casting a nervous glance at the lewd advertisements on the walls.

"Don't worry, a lot of girls your age get it. No one will question it on your file." He winked. "It is quite expensive, though."

I caught up. "Worth every penny."

Cea and I reclaimed our devices. Andes handed me his phone, and I signed off on a lengthy contract I was too nervous to read. Then I wired him the money without questioning the amount. My checking had definitely taken a hit over the past few days, but I wasn't hurting by any stretch of the imagination.

I rearranged my face into the cold, confident expression he was no doubt expecting from someone with money and power. "And what guarantee do I have that you'll fulfill your end of the bargain?"

He spread his hands. "What guarantee do you need?"

"Nic and I are very close," I said, which in some twisted irony was the truth. "Don't make me call him."

Andes stiffened, which I took as a good sign. "I wouldn't dream of it, lass."

I nodded curtly, then turned to go without another word.

Cea thanked him and hurried after me. I stepped out of the shop and heard voices—the alley that had been blissfully abandoned moments before now had a few people milling around in it. I resisted the urge to glance their way and strode towards the main road like I belonged in this part of town.

Cea caught up to me. "Good job."

I took in a deep breath—not that the air in the alley was much cleaner than the air in the shop—and hoped it would clear the anxiety out of my chest. "You sure about this guy?"

"He's your best bet for fifty miles. He's been in the business for a while—I doubt he's eager to blow it now, especially when you're willing to pay a premium. He's probably more interested in earning your loyalty so you'll bring him repeat business."

"I hope I never need his services again," I muttered, and stopped on the curb.

I glanced both ways, looking for the bus. I was eager to get out of this part of town and back to the Vons. I needed a shower and—

"Cea." I grabbed her arm.

She jerked. "What?"

I gestured with the barest nod of my head down the road.
At the end of the block stood a cop, watching us.

14

He stood in the middle of the road like he'd risen from the sewer. His stance was almost comical; his hands hung limply at his side, and a garish balloon of red-orange hair covered his head, like he was a clown posed to deliver the jump scare in a bad horror movie.

I was certainly terrified. Only one thought formulated over the roar of fear and what-if's:

We should have checked for bears.

I registered the screech of brakes and rush of air as the bus jerked to a stop. Cea yanked me back from the curb. "Come on."

I turned around and followed her down the street in the opposite direction. She walked crisply, like she had a meeting to catch. I struggled to match her stride, even though my legs wobbled like a newborn calf. *Oh Jesus, help.*

"Where are we going?"

"We're losing him."

She turned a corner, and we came upon an entrance to the subway. She scanned the square, then started down the steps.

Feeling like Lot's wife, I stole a sinful glance behind me. The cop was walking our way.

I scurried down the damp steps after Cea. "He saw us enter!"

"It won't matter in a minute." She pushed through the turnstile and merged with the crowd.

I fought to keep up with her as the smell of must and grease assaulted me with foggy memories. It had been years since I'd ridden the subway, and my anxiety was making the tunnel feel claustrophobic.

The station was a blindingly lit cave of concrete crammed with five o'clock commuters. We cut into the middle of a line, and the crowd funneled us through checkpoints that flashed green approvingly. I struggled to follow as Cea snaked her way through the throng. She shoved her way to the front just as the next train screamed to a stop at the platform. She was on before the carload of passengers had even disembarked.

It took me another minute to fight through the crowd and get on the train. Thankfully Cea had taken a seat right inside the door and saved a spot for me—despite the disgruntled looks of other passengers.

"Try to keep up next time," she whispered.

The doors whooshed shut, and the train took off with a lurch. I scanned the receding platform, but if the cop followed us into the station, I couldn't see him through the crowd.

We rode the line several stops down, then got off, waited for the next train, and immediately got back on. Then we exited the station, looped around to the northbound line, and went back the way we came. We repeated this process a few more times until I could have sworn we'd visited every station within a two-mile radius. Finally we got back on the southbound line and let it carry us to Allston.

I didn't speak until we'd emerged from the underground onto the darkening sidewalk. Cea thankfully knew exactly where we were, and we walked the rest of the way to her parents' house.

I found myself scanning the shadowy yards as we passed. "Do you think we lost him?"

She actually laughed. "We lost him thirty minutes ago. And besides—he wasn't looking for us."

I did not share her humor. "How do you figure?"

"If he was chasing us, we would have known as soon as we walked away. You have to remember—as far as he knows, we're legal citizens. We have no reason to be afraid of the cops. But you can never be too careful—which is why you should always take the subway instead of the bus if you think you're being followed."

I made a concentrated effort to stop looking behind me and stared at her instead. "How's it any safer?"

"First, it's easier to hide in a crowd. Second, even the United has trouble tracking the subway. They scan you when you enter and exit the station—but none of the platforms in between are regulated. Even if they saw us enter, they'll have to sort through the hundreds of other passengers that walked through that checkpoint during the same ten-minute window. That's why the subway is the best place to arrange a drop-off, at least around here."

We came in sight of the Vons' house, and I was surprised to find the porchlight on. I fished the key out of my backpack and let us in.

"There you are!" Mrs. Von exclaimed as we entered the kitchen. She gave Cea an annoyed look, as if she were surprised she came back, but she offered me an expression that resembled a smile. "I thought you were going to help with dinner."

"I mean... of course," I stuttered. I had told her as much before Cea and I left this morning—did she remember?

I glanced at Cea, but the nuance was lost on her. She returned her mother's glare, then stormed out of the room with a sniff that threatened to turn teary. I heard her stomp up the stairs and sent a prayer up after her.

Cea didn't come back down for dinner, so the Vons and I went through our routine. I excused myself before Mr. Von could pull me in front of the TV. I went upstairs to find Cea lying on her bed, jacket and shoes still on, as if she'd thrown herself down on the pillows and refused to get up.

"Do you want anything to eat?"

"Go sleep in Nic's room," she snapped.

"I need the radio. Dad's calling me soon." I knelt down and grabbed the box without waiting for permission.

She sighed and sat up. "I'm sorry, Phil, I just—"

"I get it." I clutched the radio to my chest and kicked the box back under the bed.

"Now you know why I never mentioned them."

I chewed my lip and gave the Holy Spirit time to speak. "Maybe it's time to start talking about it."

She glanced sideways at me. I sat down next to her on the bed. "I know it's hard, but they'll never remember you if you're never here."

"Just as well," she muttered.

"Is it?" I wondered aloud, even though I hadn't meant to.

Her expression clouded. "You saw how she looked at me, like I'm breaking and entering. I'm not their daughter anymore."

"But you are."

"You don't get it, Phil!" Tears sprang to Cea's eyes, and she tried to cover them up with violence. She yanked her shoes off and flung them into her bookcase, upending several figurines. "They're gone. I don't know who that is down there in the living room, but they're *not* my parents. My parents are dead. You have no idea what that feels like."

I waited for her to realize her error.

She washed white. "I'm sorry. I didn't—"

I folded her in a hug. I waited until her breathing had slowed before I spoke again. "I do understand. But your parents aren't dead—they're right there."

I pulled away and studied her. She stared at her hands in her lap.

I pinched her shoulder. "They *do* remember things—if you repeat them enough. She remembered I was coming back to help with dinner. I think she left the porchlight on for me."

Cea didn't appreciate the sentiment. "That's not remembering, Phil—that's habit. Of course you can program them to have habits. What do you think they were in therapy for three years for? Their entire existence is just a bunch of patterns. Right now you're part of the routine—but as soon as you leave, they'll get on without you. But that's not the same as accepting me as their daughter." She wiped her eyes. "Nic's right—Mars is where I belong. I'm going home."

I looked down at the radio in my lap and idly twisted the dials. Maybe she was right—maybe I was reading too much into Mrs. Von's actions. But I couldn't imagine leaving my parents to die, letting them rot away in their quaint suburban prison, when I knew I still had a chance.

It had been almost a decade since their surgery; neuroscience had advanced leaps and bounds since then. Surely there was some kind of therapy they could try—if only Cea or Nic would take the time to look.

"When was your dad going to call?" Cea asked, as if she knew where my train of thought was going.

I glanced at the clock. "8:30—any minute now."

I reached down to turn the radio on, but Cea laid her hand across mine.

"Let your dad know you're with me, but don't say my name on air."

I searched her face and waited.

She spoke slowly, as if trying to work it out for herself. "A lot of these people know I'm Nic's sister. If they find out you're with me… it won't take a master's degree to work out that Nic's involved somehow."

"Andes knows about Nic." I tapped my finger on the device. *And so does Aurelius.*

"Yes, but Andes has reasons to stay quiet. We don't need anyone else digging into Nic's file and finding he suddenly has a new dependent."

I nodded, once again glad I'd followed Nic's advice and kept Aurelius at a distance. *It's almost over. As soon as I can get Dad and Ephesus on their new files, I won't need Aurelius anymore.*

I turned the radio on and tuned to channel 2.

At first there was only static. I listened for one minute, two. Cea shifted beside me. I checked the time: 8:33. Did I have the wrong channel? Did he tell me the wrong time? What if something happened to him?

Take it easy... I swallowed a breath and put the handset to my lips. "Radio check."

The response was instant. "This is Catalyst, receiving."

I pinched my eyes shut in relief as the familiarity of his voice rushed through me. "This is Blue Fire."

"Good. We only have a few minutes, so listen closely." His voice was firm but comforting, so I followed his lead. "Are you in a safe place?"

"Yes." I glanced at Cea. "I have a friend with me."

"I see." A beat. "Do I know this friend?"

"Yes." I searched my memory banks, struggling to think of a mnemonic only he would know. "Remember how you said I make 'convenient' friends?"

He answered me with silence, so I tried again. "And you were glad I'd found someone who had taken a liking to me?"

"Ahh." The recognition dawned in his voice. "Is your friend safe?"

"Yes."

"Does she have her affairs in order?"

I remembered what Cea had said to Andes this afternoon and inferred what he meant. "Yes, she does."

"Does she have a safe place to go?"

"Yes."

"Good. I want you to go with her."

The receiver suddenly felt cold to the touch, as if my hand had frozen around it. "What?"

"I want you to go with her and lay low until I find you."

His voice held no uncertainty, but I could think of a million excuses. "I can't leave you."

"You have to. I need you to be safe."

Cea gave me a pointed look that I ignored. "I'm safe here, I promise."

"Not for long. Look, Blue Fire, there's more going on than you realize, things I can't discuss on here. And this time, I mean it when I say I'm not withholding this information to hurt you."

But you don't have all the information this time. "No, you don't get it. Things have changed. I have mo—"

Cea squeezed my knee sharply, so I backpedaled. "I have *resources*. I have the means to get you and Eph—Klez to a safe place if you'll just meet up with me."

I gave him a chance to argue. When he didn't, I seized my window of opportunity. "My friend helped me arrange everything. It's all in order. I just need you to make contact with me."

He prefaced his reply with a heavy breath. "Is this true?"

"Absolutely," I said, hoping the confidence was viable in my voice.

"And you're sure the place you're staying is safe?"

"Yes. I'm fine, I promise. Please don't make me leave without you."

I tried to maintain the same professionalism he had and failed as the poisonous memories came rushing back.

I won't leave you!

We don't have a choice.

"I won't go. Not this time," I whispered, tears punctuating my words. Cea slid her arm around my shoulder.

Help me, Daddy, please!

Just go. Please. Before you get hurt.

"Okay." Dad collected his nerves with a sigh. "I won't make you leave without me. But I need you to promise me that you'll stay right where you are."

"Of course." I wiped my eyes with the heel of my hand.

"Don't move. Don't hang out in public spaces. Stay off the radio. Don't go online."

"Yessir."

"I will contact you when it's safe to meet. I don't know how long that will be." The doubt crept back into his voice, and I silently begged him not to change his mind. "I need to find Klez first. I have a lead, but these things take time. It could be weeks before we can see each other."

He stressed the end of the sentence hard, and I knew he was now silently begging *me* to change my mind. But I couldn't. Not when I'd come so far—not when I had the means to save him. How was he going to get to Mars without me? He didn't have the money or the contacts to forge a file. He needed me.

"I understand, sir," I said by way of deferral.

He didn't sound pleased, but he didn't argue. "And one more thing."

I waited, receiver clenched in my hand.

"If you sense *any* trouble—feel like someone's following you, or anything compromises your position—I need you to leave. I need you to promise me that you'll buy the next available ticket and go home to your friend."

Cea rubbed my shoulder. I swallowed.

"I will find you." Dad's voice reached out to me, but the bad memories got there first.

If I come back, I will find you.

"I promise," he repeated. "You can trust me."

Philadelphia, I will not leave you.

Dad wouldn't take silence for an answer. "Promise me, Blue Fire."

Not if I have a choice.

"I promise," I whispered. *Please, God, don't make me do it.*

"Thank you." The relief in my dad's voice was palpable, and it gave me a little courage. "I need to get off now. Stay where you are and wait for me to contact you."

"How will you contact me?" I asked, scrambling for a thread of security, something to hang on to while I sat around and did nothing.

"If there's any update, I'll try to reach you on this channel, same time. You can tune your radio to listen once a night—but other than that I want you to stay off. Don't say anything unless you hear from me first."

"What if it's important?" I realized how childish that sounded, so I quantified. "Like Klez makes contact with me."

"You can try this channel. But be very careful what you say—someone is always listening. And you can't trust—" There was a blip of static, and I thought I lost him.

"Trust who? Catalyst?"

He came back in with a sigh. "I can't be more specific on here. Just remember that not everyone who calls you Blue Fire is your friend."

You don't know him. "I understand."

"Good. I'm trusting you to be smart about this. If anything happens—you feel like you're in any kind of danger—just leave. Don't try to send a message. Just go and I'll catch up with you."

Just go.

I fought to keep the emotion out of my voice. "Yessir."

"Thank you. I love you." He crammed a year's worth of affection into the phrase. "Catalyst over and out."

"Over and out," I mumbled to the room, even though I didn't bother to press down the handset. I dropped it in my lap and listened to the static, wishing the thrum would drown out my other thoughts.

Cea finally reached down and turned the radio off, bringing back the unwelcome silence. "It's not too late to change your mind. You can come with me."

"You know why I can't," I snapped, more harshly than I intended.

She graciously absorbed the bitterness. She leaned over and gave me another hug that I weakly returned. "You'll be safe as long as you stay with Mom and Dad," she said, more to convince herself than anyone else. "Just lay low. Your dad knows what he's doing."

And so do I. I have money. I can fix this. "I'll be all right. The basement really needs to be cleaned anyway." I pulled away from her and offered her a smile.

She took it. "We'll all be on Mars together again soon."

I glanced at the starry sky peeking through the blinds.

And maybe, just maybe, we would never come back.

15

"You don't have to drop me off," Cea said, probably to relieve herself of any guilt. I could tell she was glad I'd come along.

I smiled at her as we climbed onto the bus. "You'd do the same for me."

We sat near the front. It would take several transfers to get all the way to the transit station, but it was worth it to get out of the house and spend one last afternoon with Cea. The rest of my week was probably going to be spent watching TV with a man who couldn't remember what he had for breakfast—I'd take the companionship while I had it.

"Got everything?"

She patted the suitcase at her feet. "Yes—and thank you. I'll pay you back."

"Don't," I said, a bit too aggressively. "I mean, you don't have to. Nic makes a big deal out of it because he'd rather die than admit that he needed me, but you and I can be adults about it."

Cea laughed. "Fine. I'll just take you shopping when you get home."

I joined her. "Deal."

We transferred at the next stop and took an aisle in the middle. A fully armed cop got on behind us and took the row next over.

I tensed. I started to turn towards Cea, but she grabbed my knee warningly. She pulled her phone out of her pocket and typed rapidly, then held the screen out for me to see.

DON'T STARE. REMEMBER, YOU'RE LEGAL

I made a quiet noise of acknowledgment. She gave me an encouraging wink, leaned back in her seat, and started scrolling on her phone like there wasn't a man with two guns and a taser sitting less than five feet away from her.

I tried to follow suit. I unzipped my backpack and made a pretense of rooting around for the lip balm I definitely didn't need in June. I told myself over and over there was nothing to be afraid of—we weren't doing anything suspicious, and no one had recognized me yet. The cop wasn't even looking at us; he had his cap pulled down low over his eyes as he stared out the window.

Thankfully, Cea distracted me by chatting about everything and nothing. We were so engrossed in our laughter that we almost missed our last transfer and had to shout at the driver to stop. We got off, giggling—and the cop followed.

Cea ran to our transfer without looking back, so I don't think she saw him. But I keenly felt his presence as we joined the line of passengers waiting to board. Cea took the first open aisle. The cop let two or three other people board ahead of him, and then he walked to the back of the bus. I kept my eyes on my tablet as he passed.

Should I say something to Cea? I decided against it. If he was following us, pointing in his direction and whispering probably wasn't a good look. And if it was nothing, I didn't want to get her riled up. He was probably just headed to the transit station— that's the only place this bus went.

The twenty-minute drive seemed to take twice that. Finally, we arrived at the transit station, and Cea and I disembarked with the majority of the other passengers. The cop did not follow; he remained on the bus until it pulled away from the curb.

I let out my breath. *You're jumping at shadows.*

I walked Cea to her gate and made sure she had everything she needed. I bought her a snack and an ebook and then wired her some extra spending money when she wasn't looking. I was sure I'd hear about it from her (or Nic) later, but it was the least I could do.

We stopped outside of security to exchange one last hug. After a minute, I'd had my fill and started to pull away—but she wouldn't let go.

"Phil," she whispered in my ear. She hesitated, then tightened her hug. "Are you sure about this?"

I wiggled out of her grasp. "It's Andi, and I'll be fine."

She kept her hand on my shoulder. "I know, I… you ever just have a feeling that something's not right?"

I did, although I usually attributed it to the Holy Spirit. But I didn't have that feeling now.

"It'll be okay. You helped me take care of everything. I just have to sit back, watch sitcoms, and wait for Dad to call. Honestly, I'll probably be bored." I really would be, and that was honestly the most concerning thing about the whole venture. Last time I was bored, I wandered into Wing 74 and started a war.

She was still struggling. "Look, I know I sound paranoid, but… I really wish you'd come with me. I bet we can still get a ticket. I'll buy you a toothbrush."

I tried to brush it off with a laugh. "Don't be like Nic—at least not in that way."

"Nic would want you to come."

I took a step back. "Nic understands why I have to do this."

She let go of my arm. I tried to patch the bridge. "But I know who to call if I need help."

She smiled. "We're here for you—both of us."

I put on my most confident grin. "I'll see you soon."

She lifted her suitcase. "Can you relay a message for me?"

"Of course."

"If you see Ephesus, tell him I love him."

I squinted at her. "What inflection do you want me to put on that...?"

She grinned coyly. "Whatever inflection you what." She turned to go.

I stood there and waved until she had disappeared behind security. My bravado wavered as soon as she was out of sight—but probably because I didn't relish the idea of being alone again. At least this time I knew where she was, and I could call her whenever I wanted.

I sent her a goodbye text just to make myself feel better, then routed my way back to her parents' house. I squeezed into a seat on the full bus and let the dissonant chatter of a dozen strangers distract my thoughts. I tried to pray, but I couldn't figure out what to talk about. My mind felt full and empty at the same time.

My attempts at divine conversation ended when I got off the bus at the first transfer hub and saw the same cop sitting on the bench.

Don't be ridiculous, it can't be the same one. They all look the same anyway.

As if he knew my thoughts, he reached up and pulled his cap off, releasing an explosion of red-orange curls.

The cop from yesterday. And he was staring straight at me.

I ran across the lot and picked the closest bus. I had no idea what line it was, but it didn't matter. I climbed on and sat as close to the driver as I could.

The cop did not get up and follow. He did, however, lean over and talk into the handset on his shoulder.

The bus jerked away from the curb, and I grabbed the pole to keep from falling over. Surely I was overreacting. It was just a coincidence that it was the same cop, wasn't it? He couldn't be trailing me—if he was, he would have gotten off at the transit station with us. He'd have no way of knowing I'd come back to this transfer hub—

Except he did. The route to the transit station was a continual loop; it only went back and forth from this transfer hub. The cop would have known I'd come back.

And apparently he wasn't interested in Cea.

What did I do? I mentally replayed my day, trying to figure out where I had gone wrong. What had I done to arouse suspicion? Did he recognize me? Surely if he thought I was Philadelphia Smyrna he would have arrested me on the spot.

If he was chasing us, we would have known as soon as we walked away.

No, I was definitely jumping to conclusions. If I were in real trouble, he would have caught up to me already.

Besides, even if he saw which bus I got on, he'd have no way of knowing where I got off.

I mapped the route I was on and saw that it passed through downtown—perfect. There were tons of subway entrances downtown. I could get off the bus, take the subway, and lose them just like Cea had shown me.

I waited until the bus had carried me into the heart of the city and got off on a busy intersection in front of a crowded mall. *It's always easier to hide in a crowd.* I stepped into the bus shelter and pulled up my map. The closest subway station was two blocks down. *Thank you, Jesus.*

I walked to the curb and looked both ways—and there was another cop.

He sat across the road on a bench where he had a perfect view of the bus stop. He crossed his arms and stared at me, unblinking.

The crossing light turned green. I felt a rush of people push past me, but I didn't move. The light turned red again, and I was left standing alone on the sidewalk. The cop continued to stare, waiting.

I turned and ran into the mall.

I took a lap around the lower level, searching for another entrance. I finally found one on the opposite end of the building. I pushed open the first set of double doors—and froze.

Two more cops stood outside on the sidewalk, talking into their handsets.

"Hey, watch it!" An angry teen grunted at me as she tried to push past me in the doorway.

I mumbled an apology and turned around.

I joined a crowd of shoppers coming through the door and let them carry me back to the main concourse. I paused by the nearest gondola and pretended to browse the wares, running my fingers over the gaudy necklaces to hide how badly my hand was shaking.

They had the building surrounded. They were definitely looking for me.

I had to get to the subway without them seeing me. That was my only hope. Surely there was another way out of this building.

I walked to the nearest map and scanned the diagram, searching for any possible exit. No doubt they had all the street entrances blocked, but—there. The parking garage. The ramp out of the parking garage dumped onto the next street over, right around the corner from the subway station.

Would they have thought to watch the parking garage? I didn't want to walk over there and find another cop; the last place I wanted to get caught alone with a police officer was in a parking garage with no people around.

I needed someone to look for bears.

Of course, I was nowhere near a radio, so that didn't help me. *Unless...*

Aurelius had access to a radio. He could ask for me.

I glanced around the concourse, then ducked into the nearest shop and hid among the cluttered clearance racks. Pulling out my tablet, I opened the messaging app and skimmed my chat history with Aurelius. He'd slowed his roll over the past twenty-four hours, which I took as a good sign; there was nothing in his recent texts that indicated he'd heard my last conversation with Dad. Mainly he was just pleading with me not to do anything stupid—as if Nic and Cea hadn't done enough of that already—and reminding me that he was here to help.

I need your help now. But if I asked him about that intersection, he'd know where I was. I wasn't keen on giving him a pinpoint, but I wouldn't be in that intersection for long. As soon as I got on the subway, I'd be hard to find. Plus, he didn't know what I looked like anymore.

I clicked in the textbox.

I NEED YOUR HELP

I hoped he would take the bait and bypass his usual guilt-tripping.

It worked. He responded within minutes.

WHAT'S WRONG? ARE YOU OKAY?

I'M FINE. I'M JUST WONDERING IF THIS PART OF TOWN IS SAFE

I hoped he would infer the meaning. I was still trying to phrase things like socially-compliant Andromeda would.

He seemed to understand and asked for the location. I took a deep breath, hoped I wasn't making a grave mistake, and sent him the cross streets.

ARE YOU THERE RIGHT NOW?

I cringed. *Don't be like this...*

NO, IT'S FOR A FRIEND

HANG ON

A minute later, he added:

THEY'RE CHECKING. HANG TIGHT

THANKS

He tried to capitalize on the opportunity.

ARE YOU SURE EVERYTHING'S GOOD?

YEAH WE'RE COOL

WANNA MEET UP LATER?

What do you think?

THIS WEEK ISN'T GOOD FOR ME

He opted not to acknowledge that.

YEAH, THAT PART OF TOWN IS LEGIT. YOU SHOULD BE FINE

THANKS

I closed the chat before he could say anything else and walked to the parking garage.

I hovered near the door until someone entered. I stole a glance around the corner while the door was open; no cops that I could see. Taking a deep breath, I grabbed the door handle and stepped out.

I shivered in the concrete-cooled air. Pulling my jacket around me, I strode towards the opposite end as fast as I dared, trying to walk with purpose. My boots echoed disturbingly loud on the pavement. A car honked on another level, and I jumped.

You're almost there.

I slowed as I neared the exit. A van entered the garage, and I stepped up on the curb to let them pass. I pressed myself against the wall and scanned what I could see of the street.

No one, except a gaggle of women walking past with their shopping bags. I swallowed my next breath and stepped out behind them.

I followed them for a block until they crossed the street. I kept walking, tossing one more glance around me. I was alone, so I picked up my pace. The subway entrance was just a block ahead around the corner.

Almost there.

I passed the last alleyway and heard a shout.

"Blue Fire!"

I instinctively turned my head—and by then it was too late.

Two men emerged from the shadows behind a dumpster. One pointed a gun at me.

"Don't scream, or we'll shoot," he said, advancing.

Oh Lord, help.

"What do you want?" I eyed them. They definitely weren't cops; they were my age, with barely enough facial hair between them to constitute a mustache, and their weapons were at least a decade old.

The second man put his hands up. "We just want to talk. We don't want to hurt you."

I don't believe that for a second.

They took another step towards me. "We've been looking for you."

"Who's we?"

But even as the word left my mouth, I knew.

They're looking for you.

I remembered the scrambling on the radio, the strangers demanding to know where I was, and Dad's cryptic warnings. He wasn't talking about the United when he told me to be careful. He was talking about the underground.

Not everyone who calls you Blue Fire is your friend.

The underground had been looking for me this whole time.

And Aurelius had led them right to me.

Why they wanted me, I couldn't fathom, but I wasn't going to play that game. Anything that involved holding me at gunpoint couldn't be good.

"What do you want, really?" I demanded.

"We need you," the first admitted with a smile, and I didn't like the sound of that at all.

The Holy Spirit rushed at me with a burst of wisdom. I drew myself up straight. "Is that so?" I said with a coldness I did not feel. "Put the gun down and maybe I'll talk."

They exchanged a glance—too long. "I don't have all day," I hissed. "You may need me, but I definitely don't need *you*."

The second one nodded. The first looked annoyed but obeyed. He bent over to put his weapon on the ground, but apparently someone else wasn't interested in peaceful negotiations, because they shot first.

I screamed as a gun fired from farther down the alley. The bullet shattered the concrete a few feet away, grazing my arm with shrapnel.

The two guys whipped around and shouted. I didn't wait to see who the other gunman was.

I turned and ran.

I darted around the corner and pounded down the steps into the subway without looking back. The station was not nearly as crowded as I'd hoped. I stood out like a fish swimming against the current as I shoved my way through the turnstile and tried to blend in with the passengers scattered on the platform. I listened for an approaching train, but the tunnels were eerily silent. Had I just missed it?

Please hurry! I bounced unsteadily on my heels, trying to conceal the adrenaline. I kept my eye on the entrance. *Please don't follow, please don't—*

A group of people descended the stairs—just as the screech of brakes echoed down the corridor. I pushed past the person in front of me and ran to the edge of the platform. I crammed my way onto the train as soon as the doors opened, ignoring the complaints of disembarking passengers.

I fled to the far corner of the cab and collapsed on the bench. It seemed like we were stalled in the station for an eternity as a million people got off and on. Finally, the train lurched away from the platform, and I stole a glance out the window. The group on the stairs turned out to be a bunch of schoolkids. There were no cops anywhere. No one ran after the departing train, shouting.

I took a scan of the other passengers, but they were all absorbed in their own business.

The adrenaline broke. I sagged against the wall, my arms shaking in time to the rattling car. The fog of blinding terror cleared just enough for me to put my fear into words.

They were shooting at me.

My nerves seized up again. *Breathe. Breathe!* I swallowed the fear and tried to smother it with the only emotion that was stronger: Anger.

I yanked my backpack off and grabbed my tablet. My sweaty fingers slipped across the screen as I struggled to unlock it.

In some cruel irony, there were no new messages from Aurelius. This time, I initiated.

I THOUGHT YOU SAID IT WAS CLEAR

He responded immediately.

WHAT? DID SOMETHING HAPPEN?

DON'T PLAY STUPID! YOU LED THEM RIGHT TO ME!

WHAT? WHO?

Before I could even fight through my rage to come up with a reply, he sent several more messages.

ARE YOU OKAY?

WHERE ARE YOU?

TALK TO ME

I never should have talked to you.

DON'T PLAY ME! I JUST GOT SHOT AT!

The typing dots appeared and vanished again. *Why are you still talking to him?* The Holy Spirit begged me to leave it alone— just walk away before someone got hurt. But I had to see his reply. I wanted—needed—there to be a good explanation, some miraculous happenstance that could make this all go away and prove that he was still my friend.

He, of course, didn't have one.

WHAT? ARE YOU SERIOUS?

ARE YOU OKAY?

CALL ME

Then without waiting for a response, he started an audio call, which I promptly ignored. He tried again—twice—then resorted to typing.

PLEASE TALK TO ME

I SWEAR I DON'T KNOW WHAT HAPPENED

JAYDE SAID THE INTERSECTION WAS CLEAR

The world lurched to a stop at the same time the train did. I lunged forward and nearly fell off the bench. I braced my boot against the floor and waited for everything to restart. The train did. My heart didn't.

You don't know him.

He didn't seem to realize what he'd said and was waiting for my reply. I finally found the coordination to type the words.

I THOUGHT YOU WERE JAYDE

He could be anybody.
He swore.

I'M SORRY I LIED TO YOU

Use him, but don't trust him.

The typing dots appeared, but I didn't wait. I hit the drop-down and blocked him.

The chat grayed out, and his avatar went dark. I hastily closed the app and shoved my tablet into my backpack.

I felt the hot tears slide down my cheeks. I covered my face, struggling not to be a spectacle. Nic was right—he had been right all along. I didn't know Aurelius. I'd given him my location and almost gotten killed. I couldn't trust him. I couldn't trust anyone.

The underground wasn't my friend; it was the enemy. They'd come for me—and they'd surely be going after Dad next. They'd shot me on sight; they wouldn't hesitate to kill my father.

We had to get off this planet.

16

I let myself in the back door and ran up the stairs before the Vons could talk to me. I dragged the radio out from under the bed and tuned it to channel 2.

"Catalyst, come in, this is Blue Fire. Please respond."

Static. I sat down on the bed and repeated myself. "Catalyst, it's me, Blue Fire. Please come in."

It was a stab in the dark—Dad had said to use this channel if I needed to reach him, but I had no way of knowing if he was monitoring it now. But it was my only hope.

I tried again. "Emergency, emergency! Catalyst, do you copy?"

A stranger answered me. "Blue Fire, this is Data, where are you? What's your status?"

I growled under my breath. *Not now!* "Stop clogging the channel."

He wasn't deterred. "Blue Fire, we need to make contact. There's been an incident—"

I should say so! I spoke over him. "Emergency, emergency! Catalyst, come in!"

Data must have brought friends, because suddenly multiple voices started competing for bandwidth. "Someone get Green Dragon on the line!"

"All units, 10-25 Catalyst?"

"Green Dragon, I'm prepped for tracking."

"Belay that, Watts. Blue Fire, do you copy?"

I ignored them all. "Catalyst, please acknowledge!"

The voices continued to bicker—one minute, two—and I started to lose hope. I gripped the receiver with both hands. *Please, God! This is my only chance!*

"Blue Fire! What are you doing? Get off the radio, now!"

Daddy. "Catalyst, something's happened. We need to talk."

New voices jumped on the line, but Daddy spoke over them. "Then you know what to do. Leave and I'll catch up with you."

"No, you don't understand—change to channel 10."

I did it without waiting for him to acknowledge. He followed and spoke first. "Blue Fire, I told you not to send a message. I need you to get on a plane and—"

"No, listen. You can't trust these people."

He was still talking, a sure sign he hadn't heard me. "—leave tonight if you can. I'll catch up, I promise."

He paused to take a breath, and I jumped in. "Dad! Just listen! The underground—"

The other voices invaded our privacy. "Channel 15!" I shouted, and switched.

This time I spoke first. "Dad, don't speak, just listen. Something's happened. You can't trust the underground. They've been stalking me." I decided to omit the fact that I was almost murdered.

"I know they are," he responded, voice thick with worry. "That's why I need you to leave."

"You don't get it! I'm trying to tell you that *you're* not safe here!"

"It's not your job to protect me."

"Dad, things aren't how you think they are. I can help you. My..." I struggled to recall the phrase, "affairs are in order."

"Blue Fire," he snapped.

I couldn't detangle the emotion attached to the name, but I didn't care. "I've arranged for your affairs. Everything's in order and we can be out of here tomorrow. But I can't tell you on this line—I need you to call me privately."

Andes claimed his other clients wouldn't interfere—but I didn't trust anyone who would shoot me in an alley in cold blood.

There was a breath of silence—long enough for me to panic. "Dad, please, you have to trust me."

He rattled off a number.

"What?"

He repeated it more slowly—a phone number. I grabbed my tablet and wrote it down while he dictated. "Text—don't call. I'll turn my device on in exactly fifteen minutes and leave it on for five minutes. Text me what I need to know. Then turn your device off and wait. I will text you back at 21:00 to arrange a meeting. If you don't hear from me at 21:00—run."

This time, I didn't patronize him. "I won't. I'm not leaving without you."

I'll never know if he would have argued—another voice jumped onto the channel and said something I couldn't make out. I didn't wait for Dad's acknowledgment and turned the radio off.

I went to Nic's room and fished one of the smartphones out from under the floorboards. Leaving the panel ajar, I took the phone back to Cea's room. I sat down on the bed, powered on the device, and altered the settings just like Cea had shown me. Then I opened the default texting app and drafted my message.

If what Cea said was true, the United would almost certainly read my text after my activity triggered their censorship programs. Andes had said his name was fake and his number untraceable, but I still had to word the message carefully.

CALL ANDES. YOU HAVE AN APPOINTMENT, CONFIRMATION NUMBER 0422

I added the phone number from the business card, then saved the message as a draft and checked the time. I still had five minutes to wait.

My heart was racing and my fingers shaking from adrenaline, so I ran through the next steps in my mind to give my nerves something to focus on. I would bring the phone online—send the text—wait for Dad's confirmation—and then turn the phone off so they couldn't track it.

Track it! If the United looked into my activity, they'd see that the text was sent from the Vons' internet connection. I couldn't bring them into this—I had to connect to another hotspot.

I remembered what Cea said about old smartphones connecting to any signal they could find. If I got out of range of the Vons' internet, the phone should connect to the nearest cell tower instead.

I had three minutes before Dad was expecting my text. I stuffed my devices in my backpack and raced down the steps.

Mrs. Von intercepted me at the bottom of the stairs. "There you are! It's almost time to start dinner!"

I wiggled past her. "I'll be right back—I need to grab something at the gas station."

She didn't buy it. She gave me a once-over, and her eyes fell on the scratches on my arm from the shrapnel.

I pulled the sleeve of my jacket down. "I tripped on the sidewalk, it's fine."

She tipped her head to one side, as if my behavior didn't fit in a pattern she could process. "Try to be more careful…"

I threw her an apologetic smile and raced out the back door.

I jogged down the street towards the bus stop. I had no intention of getting on, but at least I wouldn't look like an idiot for running towards it. I reached the bench just when fifteen minutes had passed. I brought the phone online, sent the text, and said a prayer.

The response was instant.

GOT IT

I wanted to say more but knew we couldn't risk it. I sent another text to Andes's number and told him to expect a call for appointment 0422. I didn't get a response, but I wasn't worried. I powered the device off and hid it in my backpack. Then I decided I'd better go to the gas station and buy something, just in case Mrs. Von was having a good day and remembered.

She didn't—but she was nonetheless pleased with the chocolate I brought her. She commandeered me as kitchen help as soon as I walked in the door, and I was grateful. It would be over four hours before I'd hear from Dad, and I wouldn't know how to contain my nervous energy otherwise.

I kept telling myself it was going to be all right. I had everything set up and in order. Dad's temporary identity was paid for, and neither the underground nor the United had any idea what was going on. As soon as Dad's new file was online, I could buy us transit tickets and we'd be on the next flight to Mars.

We still had to find Ephesus, but Nic was right—Ephesus was a grown man. He'd been smart and not gotten tangled up with the underground; he wasn't in immediate danger, not like Dad. Once we got back to base, I could go back to looking like Philadelphia and record videos again. Ephesus would see them.

I excused myself from the living room at 8:30 and went upstairs to pack. I put my clothes and makeup in the suitcase and left it on the bed, then took my tablet off the charger. I glanced at the messaging app and realized I'd missed a notification from Nic—he was asking if Cea had left.

I responded with an affirmative, then debated letting him know we were coming. After a minute, I decided against it. He would *not* be pleased when he heard about the risk I was taking, and I didn't want him asking questions until our itinerary was set in stone. No use ruffling his feathers when it wouldn't change anything.

I slung my backpack over my shoulder and left out the back door, trying to be quiet and not disturb the Vons.

I walked to a different bus stop this time, one a few blocks over, so they wouldn't pinpoint my burner phone to the same location. It was long past dark, and the street was comfortably deserted except for some kids hanging out in front of a gas station down the way. I sat down on the bench under the streetlight and powered on the smartphone.

8:58—still early. Andes had responded to my text with a thumbs up a few hours ago, which I took as a good sign. 8:59. I checked to make sure my connection was good and refreshed the app.

9:00. Nothing yet—but clocks could be off. I waited three more minutes. Still nothing.

I decided to initiate.

YOU GOOD?

I waited several more minutes. No response.

I checked my connection again. I had full bars.

If you don't hear from me at 21:00—run.

No—I wasn't going to leave him behind just because he was five minutes late texting me. I already told him I wouldn't go.

9:08. I got up and started walking. If the United was tracking my signal, I needed to be a moving target.

I walked another three blocks down the road. 9:15.

Maybe his appointment with Andes was running long. It had taken a couple of hours to get my prints altered—if Andes hadn't gotten him in until later in the day, Dad might still be tied down in the machine and couldn't text back.

I dialed Andes's number. He picked up immediately and barked a gruff greeting that was probably Scottish.

"Andes, we spoke earlier. I set up the appointment for 0422."

"Lass!" His bellow filled the line. "All good on your end? I'm still waiting."

"What?" The sound came out more breath than word.

"Your man hasn't showed. Did you give him the right number? If he calls I can give directions."

I hung up.

17

I dialed Dad's number. It rang through—but that meant the phone was on, wasn't it?

I tried again. It rang only three times before sending me to voicemail. I switched back to text.

ANDES SAID YOU DIDN'T SHOW. WHERE ARE YOU?

No response.

I dialed again. This time it cut me off on the first ring—and a text immediately came through.

It was an address.

I mapped it on my tablet and was relieved to see that it was only ten minutes away by bus.

Another text came through.

THIRD FLOOR. HURRY

I powered off the smartphone and started running.

I darted across the street to catch the bus heading in the other direction. Thankfully the lines were still running, and the next bus was due within minutes. I practically fell into the road waving the driver down as he came around the corner.

I took the first seat, not caring that it was marked for the elderly. The bus zoomed towards the outskirts of town, and I prayed there would be no one waiting at the other stops so that we'd get there faster.

Oh God, please let him be alive! Please let me get there in time!

The address took me to a shell of an office building on the edge of town. It was vacant, the dusty for sale sign in the window sending up a weak S.O.S. All of the windows were dark, and several had been bashed in.

I would have thought I'd come to the wrong place if the front door weren't propped open.

I ran inside and scanned the lobby. No one was in sight. There was no power to the elevator, so I found the emergency stairs and raced to the third floor. The only lights in the stairwell were the emergency exit signs, and I tripped three times in the dark.

I shoved open the door to the third floor. It dragged on its hinges with a hideous squeak like I'd raised it from a dead sleep.

A quick scan of the floor made it appear empty except for the frames of abandoned cubicles and a couple of bereaved desks. The halls in every direction were dark; the only light came from the glare of the streetlamp outside the bay windows that lined the wall on the left.

"Dad?" I called, and my voice echoed back to me hollowly. I crept down the left side of the room, staying close to the light. I tensed as I passed each cubicle, expecting the worst—but it never came. There was no sound, no movement, no evidence that anyone had been here in months.

I reached the opposite end of the room and peered into the dark hallway beyond. "Dad?" I tried again.

At first, silence—then the most sickening sound I could have imagined: muffled shouting, and the smacking of a hand on glass.

"Dad!" I ran. I looked in every office I passed, searching for any sign of life. Finally, I saw a faint blue glow flickering from around the corner up ahead. The shouts came again, closer this time, and I thought I heard my name.

"I'm coming!" I stumbled around the corner into an empty lab. Most of the equipment had been swept away into the corners to die, but one machine was alive and throbbing. It was a hefty glass-and-metal tube, propped up at an angle. And my dad was trapped inside.

I screamed. He saw me and banged on the glass, shouting something that was still too muffled to hear. I ran to him, tripping once on the way there, and collapsed against the side of the machine.

"Are you okay? What happened? Who did this to you?" I pressed myself against the cold glass and searched his face for answers. He seemed alert, his eyes wild and dilated. There was a smear of blood on the inside of the glass that matched the small wound on his forehead. But otherwise he seemed unhurt.

He put his palms against the glass to match mine. "Philadelphia, listen to me." His words chattered along with his teeth, and his breath clouded the air inside the tube, briefly making him invisible.

"What is this thing?" I stepped back and scanned the machine. The tube itself was little more than a glass coffin with a single keypad on the side, but it was hooked to several other machines and a flashing control panel by a tangle of wires. A thick hose ran out the back and connected the tube to a large metal canister. I didn't recognize the chemical symbols on the side, but I didn't like the look of it—or the fact that the whole apparatus was absolutely *freezing.* My fingers grew numb against the frosty glass, but I refused to move.

"We have to get you out of here."

"The control panel," he said. I touched the keypad on the side of the tube, and he gestured wildly. "No, the computer. Abort the process." He coughed, as if those words had taken all the breath left in his lungs.

What process? I didn't have the stomach to ask. I turned to the control panel and swiped through the open menus, looking for anything with a "stop" button or red X. Everything was timers and readouts and nothing I could control.

Oh, God, help. "I can't find—"

"Philadelphia!" My father's voice changed pitch into a shriek.

I turned my head—right into the barrel of a gun.

Before I could even process what I was seeing, someone grabbed me from behind. The gun was rammed under my chin, scaring away any cry that attempted to leave my lips.

"Hello, Philadelphia," my captor said by way of greeting.

My heart was beating too loudly in my skull for me to identify the voice. Thankfully he put his lips close to my ear and repeated himself. "Not so clever now, are we?"

Carnegie. I daren't turn to look, but in my peripheral I could see the wrinkled hand holding the gun and knew it was him.

"Carnegie, please don't hurt her." My father fought to keep his voice level even as it shook from exhaustion. He struggled to stay upright. I could see now that he was turning white and blue in all the wrong places.

Carnegie savored the spectacle. "You had your chance for peaceful negotiations—twice now. Although I suppose I can't really blame you for the fiasco on Rott." His strangely warm hand fingered my neck.

I resisted the urge to swallow. "What do you want?"

He barked a laugh. "I have what I want. What I would *love* is to kill you right now and let you bleed out while he watches."

He jammed the gun into my throat, causing me to gag. My dad made an unutterable cry of agony. I pinched my eyes shut.

Jesus Jesus Jesus.

"But." Carnegie loosened his hold, and I sucked in a gasp of air. "Revival is expensive, so I suppose we could still make a deal."

Revival? Somehow I knew he wasn't talking about church.

He turned back to my dad. "Give me Red Rain, and I'll let her live."

Dad didn't even flinch, but I felt my soul freeze over. *No. Not again.*

"I'll put her under for a week—just so there's no incidents—and if you give me the formula, you can both go free. I'll even buy you a transit ticket to Mars as a gesture of goodwill." I felt the chuckle vibrate in his chest. "You can tell Nic I sent you."

Dad's eyes flickered back and forth between me and Carnegie.

"Well, doctor? What will it be?" Carnegie taunted, twisting the gun against my throat.

Dad opened his mouth—but I spoke first.

"No."

Carnegie dug his fingernails into my neck, but I ignored him. I swallowed and straightened as best I could. "We won't do it."

"I wasn't asking you." His spit landed on my ear.

I flinched. "And I wasn't talking to you." I met my dad's gaze and held it with all the conviction and sincerity I could muster. "Don't let him win."

Help me, Dad. Fight with me.

His face was pinched in an expression I couldn't interpret. I kept going. "My life isn't worth millions of others."

"It is to me," he said, voice clogged with a lifetime of heartbreak. He coughed again. Carnegie laughed cruelly.

I jerked against him to shut him up. "I know, but this is what's right."

Don't let them use you. Don't let them blackmail you.

Dad didn't argue. He put both palms flat against the glass, even as they trembled.

"This is my choice," I said. The adrenaline sapped the courage from my voice, but I kept speaking from the conviction I knew was hiding under the blinding roar of death.

Whatever they tell you, whatever they say they're going to do to me, don't listen.

"Don't do it. Don't give him Red Rain."

Don't let him win.

"I will drop her right here and now," Carnegie said, as if there was any doubt. "And I'll be happy to make it slow and painful. So make your choice, doctor."

Dad closed his eyes and leaned his bloody forehead against the glass. I saw his lips moving and followed suit.

With great effort, Dad pushed himself upright. When he opened his eyes again, he focused them straight at Carnegie.

"I won't do it." His voice still quavered from the cold, but it had the strength of a thousand men. "I won't give you Red Rain."

I smiled at him through my tears.

Thank you, Jesus.

Carnegie made a noise of annoyance. He hesitated, and for a brief moment hope shot through me. Had we called his bluff?

Then he adjusted his grip on the gun and regained control of the situation. "Well, at least that answers one question."

Neither I nor my father replied. The terror returned to my father's face as he realized what he'd done.

I heard the smile in Carnegie's voice. "Thank you for letting me know your daughter is expendable."

Dad uttered an oath. I closed my eyes and braced myself for the inevitable that never came.

"But luckily for you, I hate her," Carnegie clenched his hand around my throat, "more than I hate you, so I'm going to let her watch you die—instead of the other way around."

Before I could comprehend what he meant, he lowered the gun just long enough to punch a button on the screen. The machine kicked into high gear. He pressed the gun to my neck again and dragged me back a few steps so I had an agonizingly clear view of the horror that was unfolding.

The machine throbbed. The pipe on the back went stiff as the canister drained its chemical contents into the line.

Dad yelled. I turned my attention back to him and saw that the glass tube was filling with liquid. It was thick and slimy and the horrid blue-green shade of evil. It crawled up the side of the tube—too fast to stop, but slow enough to send Dad to hell in his own mind. I almost vomited as all the emotions of a man facing death contorted his face. He rammed his fists, then his shoulder, over and over into the glass, but it did nothing.

I sobbed and fought against Carnegie, but he held me back.

The liquid reached Dad's neck. In panic he threw one last plea towards Carnegie. "Please—"

Whatever he was going to say was drowned out as he swallowed a mouthful of liquid. He thrashed as he went under. There was a flash of light and a hideous crack—and then silence.

Carnegie released me. I stumbled forward and crashed into the machine, swiping furiously at the frost that clouded the glass. But no matter how hard I wiped, all I could see was a solid block of greenish ice inside the tube.

"You killed him!" I screeched, but the sound came out garbled like a strangled animal.

"Not exactly." Carnegie approached from behind and tapped the control panel. "He's frozen for safekeeping. When I'm ready to use him, I'll bring him back."

I snarled. I whipped around to punch him, but he was ready. My punch bounced weakly off his arm, and then he reached out to trip me.

I landed hard and struggled to get up, but he kicked me sharply under the ribs. I wailed.

"Oh, Philadelphia, you know this is all your fault, right?"

I squinted at him through the tears.

He kicked me again. "You led me right to him."

I scrambled backwards until I was in the middle of the floor. He just watched me and smiled. "I knew you wouldn't listen to Nic. I knew you couldn't sit still. And when I gave you that scare in the alley—I knew you'd pull the trigger and flush my fox out in the open."

The world was spinning in time to the pain that was radiating through my body. I pushed myself up on one knee and fell down again. "I don't—that was you?"

He spread his hands, face consumed in a proud grin. "Those cops work for me. I've been following you this whole time, Philadelphia—or should I say, *Andromeda*."

I managed to stand even though I was shaking uncontrollably.

He answered my unspoken question. "Of course I knew. It was part of my deal with Thames—he gave me my weapons, and I gave him the daughter he always wanted. Shame he never got to claim his prize."

Carnegie's laugh filled the room along with the thunderous roar of my guilt.

He's right. This is all your fault.

He checked to make sure his gun was still loaded and ready. Then he aimed it at me. There was nowhere to run—he stood between me and the hallway.

"You should have stayed on Mars, sweetheart."

You should have listened to Nic.

Carnegie put his finger on the trigger—and someone else fired.

The deafening explosion ripped the scream from my throat. Carnegie lurched forward one drunken step, planting his foot as if he could save himself by keeping his balance. His eyes flashed, then glazed. He coughed blood.

Then he collapsed face first on the concrete, a bullet lodged in his back.

Stanyard stood behind him, panting.

A pistol smoked in his hands. He kept it aimed, hands steady despite the shaking of his chest, as if he expected Carnegie to come back for more. The room was silent except for the ringing in my ears. We both stared at Carnegie until the amount of blood seeping through his lab coat made his state of life clear.

Stanyard finally looked at me, eyes burning. "What do you think you're doing?" he yelled, more colorfully than necessary. "Why didn't you call for help?"

He was shouting—and he sounded very, very angry.

"Call for help?" I squeaked. I wasn't sure whether to be afraid, offended, or confused—and then I realized I was all three with a vengeance. "How could I have called for help? I didn't even know you were *alive*." My volume rose to match his.

He put his hands up. "I'm sorry. I'm sorry. I'm sorry." With each repetition, he lowered his voice until it was an acceptable level. He swiped at the sweat on his forehead. "I just… I thought I lost you again."

His words ricocheted around the lab, louder and more terrifying than the gunshot. My ears started ringing again, and I remembered.

I thought I lost you.

I'm sorry, Phil, I really am.

I'm sorry I lied to you.

I took a step back, feeling sick and unsafe all over again. "It was you. Aurelius—that was you the whole time."

He looked down, but only for a beat before he lifted his eyes to meet mine. He nodded.

I tried to attach an emotion to that revelation and failed. I would have taken any emotion—fear, anger, betrayal. Any concrete feeling would have been better than the swirling pressure in my chest, like a vacuum had been created that was sucking out my ability to process and breathe and be my own person.

"You lied to me," I finally managed, but it did nothing to direct the storm.

He nodded again.

"Why? Why not just tell me?"

It was a genuine question—the correct answer to which could have reset the universe. Unfortunately, he didn't have a good answer.

"You said yourself you didn't trust me," he mumbled.

You're right, I don't.

Suddenly, a recognizable emotion formed in my throat, and I grabbed it. "You almost got me killed!" I screeched.

"I swear I don't know what happened. Jayde said—"

"I thought you were Jayde!" Suddenly, icy fear clashed with the anger burning in my veins like lava meeting water. "Does he know? Where is he? What did you do to him?"

"Whoa." Stanyard slid back. "Jayde's fine. What, you think I'd hurt him?"

Well, you hurt me. "I don't know what to think," I said, which was the truth.

Stanyard searched my face. He didn't look offended, as if he'd seen this coming all along. "Jayde's safe. He's back with the others. And yes, he knows. He was with me the whole time."

"Oh, so you all agreed to lie to me." I wanted to be angry about that too, but suddenly I just felt *tired.* Stanyard had lied to me *again*, and Jayde had lied to me, but then they'd both come back and tried to save me, and then Stanyard had just now *actually* saved me, and apparently we were all going to be together again.

All of these things seemed important, and yet not important, and meanwhile Carnegie was still lying on the floor between us, dead and getting deader.

Stanyard didn't wait up for my mental composure. "Look, can we talk about this later? We need to get out of here. Whoever he's working for—" He shook his pistol at Carnegie, "—knows you're here. As soon as they realize he's gone dark, they'll have this place surrounded."

He took a step towards me, and suddenly I remembered who else was in the room. "Dad!"

I ran to the machine. Stanyard turned to follow and muttered an oath. "Did he—?"

"He's frozen," I stated the obvious. I swiped more frost from the glass, then instantly regretted it. Dad's face was faintly visible through the block of solid cryoprotectant. He floated eerily, like he was suspended a few inches under a frozen lake.

The rapid process had turned his fear into a stone monument—his eyes screaming in terror, mouth agape, body twisted in pain.

A sound I couldn't remember summoning wrenched out of me.

Oh God.

Stanyard approached the tube slowly and looked in. "Oh Phil," he breathed. "I'm sorry."

I muttered in tongues under my breath, then swallowed the rush of courage. "We have to get him out. Help me." I reached for the control panel.

"Don't touch that!" Stanyard lunged forward, hand reaching to block mine—then realized he was still holding a gun. He quickly set the safety and stuffed it in the belt of his jeans. "You can't just thaw him out—that's not how that works."

I stared at him, my heart racing again—this time in tune to an entirely new breed of panic.

"There's a whole process to thawing someone out. It's not like defrosting a turkey—you can't just let them come to room temperature. He'll need neurotherapy and blood transfusions and a bunch of stuff."

"But he's only been frozen for a minute!"

"Doesn't matter! We're going to have to take him to a reviving facility."

"But I can't just leave him here." I couldn't leave him—not after I'd just found him—and if Carnegie had people, they would surely be coming. I wouldn't let them have Dad, frozen or otherwise.

Stanyard knelt and rooted around on the floor. "You won't have to." There was a grunt, and he stood up. "This is a mobile transport tube. It can be unplugged for several hours." He held up a thick, multi-pronged cord for emphasis.

The display on Dad's tube chirped and changed color. It glowed yellow, and a timer started counting down from three hours. I watched the seconds tick, then glanced back up at Stanyard.

"Carnegie wasn't planning on keeping your dad here," he said.

I swallowed. "I know." Where would he have taken him? Had he found more allies? Who was he working with?

Stanyard started disconnecting the other hoses and wires that anchored the tube to the machine. "The other guys are on their way—I sent them my location. They can move him."

"I'll wait with him."

"No, you won't." A pipe hissed at him as he released the seal. "Phil, if they find out you're still alive, they'll either finish the job, or they'll take you who-knows-where. We need to get you out of here, now."

"But Dad—"

"The guys will take care of him. Please, just come with me." He pulled out the last plug and turned to extend a hand to me.

I stared at it, his palm streaked with sweat and gunpowder, and suddenly I was back in that dreaded alley as he reached to help me out of the car.

Phil, if you don't come now, I'll leave you behind!

I could tell by the look in his eyes that he was there too. He dropped his hand and wiped it on his jeans. "This way. The car's out back."

He started walking. With one last glance back at Dad, I followed.

18

Stanyard mercifully stayed silent as he drove us back to base. I spent the ride gripping the passenger door handle, trying not to choke on residual adrenaline. It didn't help that my muscles had memorized what happened the last time I'd ridden in a car with Stanyard.

"Base" ended up being a nondescript brick-and-steel office building, not unlike Thames's headquarters. What surprised me was that it was located smack-dab in the middle of a busy thoroughfare on the fringes of downtown.

Stanyard answered my quizzical stare with a shrug. "It's easier to hide in plain sight."

He drove underneath the building into the parking garage. Jayde stood in the middle of the lot, waiting for us.

He opened my door as soon as Stanyard parked. "Blue Fire! You made it! We all thought you were going to go dark."

I almost did. I got out and studied him, trying to decide if I was happy to see him or not.

He didn't wait for an emotional reaction. "I owe you an apology."

That was a cold open I couldn't ignore. I shifted my eyes to his face.

He returned my stare. "Those men that stopped you in the alley this afternoon? They were my guys."

"What?" I yelled—or tried to yell. The word caught on my throat, raw from processing death and terror, and came out weak and raspy.

He nodded. "We've been trying to find you since you came back to Earth. Stanyard was our only contact, and when you kept ghosting him, I realized I'd have to do it the old-fashioned way. Stanyard radioed to ask if that intersection was clear, and I figured this was my only chance. I sent guys to pick you up. You almost fooled them with your new look—but thankfully you answered to your name."

My fists and jaw tightened again. I had a dozen questions—and I suspected none of them had good answers. "So you were going to kidnap me?" I put several steps between us and wondered—yet again—if I'd made a mistake going with Stanyard.

Jayde put his hands up. "No, but you weren't safe out there."

"I was doing just fine until your guys nearly got me killed!" *Dad was right about you. You're not my friend.*

"We didn't know Carnegie was trailing you too!" He raised his voice, as if shouting over my panic would fix it. "If I had known—"

"What? You would have sent your goons to stalk me another day?" I couldn't decide whether I wanted to throw up or start running. I glared at Stanyard, who stood several feet away. "How could you? You said—"

"He didn't know!" Jayde lunged between us. He stopped, took a deep breath, and forced his voice back down to a normal level. "I told him that intersection was safe. He didn't know I had guys out looking for you. Be mad at me if you want, but he wasn't involved, I swear."

The disgusted look on Stanyard's face suggested that was the truth, so I accepted it.

"I know you think I'm a creep," Jayde drew my attention back to himself, "but I think you'll forgive me when you see who's inside waiting for you."

My heart rammed against my chest. "Ephesus," I whispered, and desperately hoped it was true.

Jayde grinned. I shoved past him and raced for the elevator. Both boys ran to catch up and barely made it before the doors closed. Jayde called level six, and I braced myself against the wall as we shot upwards. I was already shaking and crying and didn't care what either of them thought.

The doors beeped and opened. I shoved my way through and ran down the hall, screaming. "Ephesus! Ephesus!"

My name echoed back to me from the far end of the hall. "Philadelphia!" He stepped out of a room. His right arm was in a cast, his hair had been buzzed short, and he had a lumpy bandage over his nose. But it was him.

I screeched and collapsed into him. He sat down on the floor and pulled me into his lap like he had when I'd found him on Mars. He rocked me with his good arm as I released all the terror of the past few weeks in an unending stream.

"Philadelphia," he whispered when I'd slowed down enough to hear him. His voice was nasally but gentle. "It's okay. You're okay."

"No it's not!" My tears returned with a vengeance when I realized I had to tell him what I'd done. "Dad—he's—I can't—" I gasped for breath.

Ephesus jerked his head up and looked at Stanyard. "He's frozen," Stanyard admitted. "Carnegie vitrified him. The guys are bringing him back now."

I felt Ephesus stiffen and cried harder. "Ephesus—I'm sorry—it's all my—"

"It's not your fault, Phil," Stanyard interrupted. "I should have told you who I was."

He should have, but would that have prevented anything? Carnegie was already watching. It was only a matter of time before he caught up to me.

Ephesus kept his arm around me protectively. "And Carnegie is…?"

Stanyard just nodded. I swallowed another sob.

Ephesus set me upright. "We'll fix this. Dad's not dead—we can bring him back. We just need a revival tech."

I nodded rapidly and rubbed both eyes with the heels of my hands. *Please, God, please. Help me fix this!*

Ephesus brushed my sweaty hair out of my face. "Did he hurt you?"

The bruise under my ribs was throbbing, but it seemed inconsequential. I shrugged and turned the questions on him. "Are you all right? Cea said—"

He gripped my arm. "Cea? You've seen her? Where is she?"

"She's safe—she's on a transit back to Mars right now." *Where you should be.*

Relief brought some color back to his cheeks. He let go of my arm. "Mars? So it's true about Nic. He's back on base."

I nodded, then remembered that no one else was supposed to know about Nic. "How did you find out?"

"They told me." He gestured with his bandaged elbow at Stanyard and Jayde.

I glanced at them and realized I was missing a big piece of the story. "Why didn't you tell me you'd found Ephesus?"

Stanyard raised his hands. "I just picked him up this afternoon."

I frowned at my brother.

He nodded to corroborate the story. "I've been in the area for the past several weeks, trying to make contact with Dad. I knew my file was flagged, and something was going on in the underground—so I was trying to avoid letting anyone know I was here. But when I overheard your last conversation, I knew something bad had happened—so I took a risk and ordered pizza."

Stanyard's lips twitched.

Something wasn't adding up. "If you knew I was in trouble, why didn't you come? Why'd you send—"

"Stanyard was closer," Jayde answered. "He was at my apartment across town—a good five miles closer to where you were. There was no way any of us would have made it in time."

"Besides," Ephesus tapped his cast, "this is my shooting arm. I couldn't have fought Carnegie in this condition."

I shuddered, finally remembering to be grateful. *You saved me, Jesus.* I looked up at Stanyard and focused on his face for the first time in several minutes. "Thank you."

He shook his head. "I wasn't fast enough. Had I figured out where that bus line was going—"

"Wait. How'd you know I was on the bus?" I sat up straight and turned to face them. "How did you know where to find me?"

He met my gaze and spoke slowly. "I was tracking Andromeda's file."

My blood ran cold as the last fragment of my privacy was ripped from my grasp. "How long have you known?"

"When you told your dad your 'affairs were in order,' I realized you must be using new credentials."

I remembered the harsh tone of voice Dad had used when I'd said it and writhed. *What have I done? How many other people know?*

But wait—just because they knew I had a new file didn't mean they knew what name it was under. "How did you figure out I was Andromeda?"

He opened his mouth, and someone else spoke.

"I told him."

I froze. I knew that voice—and she was the last person I wanted to see right now.

Stanyard glanced over his shoulder and stepped aside.

Mrs. Nolan stood at the end of the hall.

"Hello, daughter."

TO BE CONTINUED...

AURELIUS
RED RAIN #3.5
RACHEL NEWHOUSE

My world ended when I saw Philadelphia in the back of the van, cuffed and unconscious.

It was noon when I got the call for two emergency pickups. This was nothing unusual—it was my job, after all. That's why I ran a takeout-only pizza shop. The frequent deliveries were the perfect cover for transporting people who had gotten themselves on the United's bad side.

Cea—or Ceasar, as I knew her—was the one to make the call. I'd been in contact with her off and on over the past few months. She'd been stirring the waters, making a name for herself and figuring out who her friends were, so I knew it was only a matter of time before she needed a pizza.

What I didn't know was that she and I had a history together.

Jayde, our mutual contact, wasn't forthcoming with this information either. Jayde was my first connection with the underground, and we'd worked together enough that we might almost call each other friends. My shop was the closest pickup and dropoff point to the office were Jayde worked. And since Jayde was a guard for a high military official, he was involved in plenty of shenanigans that required pizza delivery.

I hadn't shared a lot of my past with Jayde, but he knew enough to realize that Cea and I had come from the same unassimilated concentration camp. You'd think he would have put two and two together and had the decency to give me a head's up that I might actually *know* the people he was depositing on my doorstep.

Instead, I was wholly unprepared when he opened the back of the van and I saw Philadelphia lying there.

I recognized her instantly, even though she was blindfolded. Her long brown hair pooled around her head like spilled coffee. She wore her favorite outfit—a khaki skirt and gray jacket with leggings and combat boots. It was the same outfit she'd been wearing when I saw her last, the day I left camp for good.

Take their offer while you still can, Phil—take it and run.

The memory of her face—watery eyes begging me to turn around and change my mind—brought with it several other images I was unprepared to handle. My parents, the commander's gun pointed at my chest, Mira, the callous goodbye note taped on our bathroom mirror—everything I had spent the last several months trying to bury came rushing back with all the requisite unwelcome emotions.

You denied Him.

Jayde was unappreciative of my existential crisis. "C'mon, man, we've gotta move!" He'd already uncuffed Cea and helped her down from the van.

I nodded, sweeping the emotions back into the corner of my mind. Jayde knelt next to Philadelphia and removed the cuffs, and I picked her up.

As her dead weight settled in my arms, I saw the dried tears on her face and was slammed with two unsettling realities:

One, she had been through hell.

Two, a *lot* had gone down since I'd left camp.

Jayde helped me get the girls into the bunker, then made himself scarce. The bunker was a concrete cellar under the shop's basement and the one part of the building the government didn't know existed. It was where all my deliveries waited until they could catch a ride somewhere else.

Somehow I had the feeling I couldn't just load Philadelphia on the produce truck and ship her back out of my life.

I laid her out on a blanket in the corner of the bunker, then took care of Cea. I got her a first aid kit and water, and she gave me the rundown while she cleaned and bandaged her own wounds.

The short of it was that Philadelphia's dad, Dr. Smyrna, had been summoned to Mars to work for Cea's brother, Dr. Nic, and gotten tangled up in a weapons plot. Now the United wanted the project finished, and they had been holding Cea and Philadelphia hostage to blackmail the scientists into completing the weapon.

The long of it was that Philadelphia's brother Ephesus, whom we all thought was dead, apparently *wasn't*, and the project was a world-ending superweapon called "Red Rain," and Philadelphia had blown up a lab and turned Nic over to the authorities, and now the United wanted the weapon for themselves, and Jayde's boss, Director Thames Nolan, was overseeing the project.

Luckily for all involved, Cea knew how to order pizza.

None of this really surprised me, except maybe the part about Ephesus coming back to life and definitely the part about Philadelphia blowing up a lab by herself.

I watched her sleep from across the room and wondered if she was the same girl I had left behind.

AVAILABLE NOW!

CATALYST
RED RAIN #4.5
RACHEL NEWHOUSE

I laughed when she said she was Catholic.

It was outlandish. In a world where being even a casual Christian was social suicide, going the extra mile and being Catholic felt flamboyant.

But even funnier was the way she said it, like she was crying *"Leprosy! Unclean!"* in the marketplace. She hadn't even offered her name; as soon as she saw me approach, she turned around and threw up that verbal stop sign, palms forward. It was like she was giving me every possible reason to reject her before I even asked her to prom.

I guess the way I sidled up her table at lunch made my intent clear.

I grinned and sat down across from her, slinging one leg over the bench. "Yeah? Well, I'm Pentecostal, which if you ask the Baptists is just as bad."

She returned my smile and lowered her hands. "Sorry, I just... don't like to lead people on."

I doubted she had ever done anything of the sort, but I knew what she meant. I was three rejections into my search for a prom date, and of the three, I thought two of them *were* Christian.

Apparently they weren't Christian enough to want to be seen with me. Word had gotten out about the marks I'd gotten on my file for praying for people in the hallway, and it was making it royally hard to find a prom date.

Perhaps an ardent Catholic would be daring enough to give me a chance.

I offered her my hand. "Well, now that we got that out of the way... I'm Thomas."

It was her turn to laugh as she accepted the shake. "Abigail."

I held her hand for an extra half-beat to preface my offer. "Can I take you to prom, Abigail?"

She didn't hesitate. "No."

I was surprised at the amount of rejection that steamrolled through my body. After all, she hadn't been my first choice for a date. But as my palms began to sweat and all the other uncomfortable symptoms of puberty radiated through me, I realized how much I was hoping she'd say yes.

I tried to play it cool. "Why not? Did you get a better offer?"

She snorted. "No."

"Aha! Then that means I'm the best offer."

She whipped her head around, as surprised as I was by my forwardness.

There was a beat, long enough that I wondered if I'd shot myself in the foot—and then she relaxed and put her chin in her hand. "Maybe you are."

My pride might have imagined it, but I could have sworn she gave me a once-over with her eyes. I wasn't chiseled; I cared too much about my grades for that. But I was lean, and just tall enough, and I'd bothered to put gel in my dark hair this morning. Apparently that, combined with my crisp button-up, was doing it for her.

The flattery gave me my courage back. I propped my elbow on the table and leaned towards her. "Well, since I'm currently the highest bidder, is there anything I can do to tempt you to change your mind? Flowers?"

She arched one eyebrow.

"Chocolate?"

Both eyebrows went up.

"Convert to Catholicism?"

She stopped, leaned back, and opened her mouth. I could tell I was about to seal the deal—before a whiny voice interrupted us.

"Hey, who's this guy?"

Abigail audibly rolled her eyes as a wiry nerd of a middle schooler joined us at the table. I could barely see his face under his mess of unkempt dark hair, but I vaguely recognized him as someone from a few grades below us.

Abigail patronized him with a sigh. "He's fine, Bart. I said he could sit here." She hadn't actually said that—because I hadn't asked—but I took the compliment.

"Bart, eh?" I said, trying to be a gentleman. "Is that short for something?" I offered my hand.

He stared at it like it was a dead fish. "For *you*, it's short for Tower."

It was a lame comeback, made even lamer by the squeak hormones put in his voice, but I wasn't about to let a twelve-year-old friendzone me. "Tower? What's that, your streamer name?"

"Obviously."

Abigail flicked her hand like he was a fly she could shoo away. "He plays this dumb game with a goat. It doesn't even have a storyline."

He *tched* and tossed his hair, which flopped around like a wet mop. "That's because it's a *physics simulator*, and I have twenty thousand subscribers now. Unlike 'Blue Fire,' who has, like, ten." He jerked his thumb at Abigail.

I arched an eyebrow at her. "'Blue Fire'?"

"Never mind, I don't even play." She coughed to clear the flush from her cheeks, then turned her frown on Bart. "Don't you have a remedial language class after lunch?"

It was his turn to blush, which made his eyes look even more sunken. "Mom wasn't supposed to tell you…"

"She told me so that I could make sure you did it. Now go."

He threw another sour glance at me, as if I was the cause of his misery, and sulked off.

"Sorry, little brothers." Abigail turned back to me with a shrug.

"Occupational hazard." I grinned, not that I had any idea what it was like to have siblings. My only brother had died in the war in Asia before I was old enough to appreciate him, but I wasn't going to burden her with my sob story. "You were telling me when mass was."

Her eyebrows returned to their locked and upright position. "You were serious about that?"

"Depends on how serious you are about not going to prom with me."

She weighed me with a sharp gaze, then reached into her backpack and fished out her phone. "What's your number?"

I was so stunned that I forgot what my digits were. After leaving her hanging for an awkward moment, I pulled myself together and took my phone out of my pocket. I held it out to her so she could tap the back and get a download of my file.

She fidgeted with a strand of her long hair. "Ahh, that feature doesn't work on mine. It's... old."

I could clearly tell that her device wasn't old, which meant the only other explanation was that it was unregistered.

"Well, aren't you full of surprises," I said with a grin. Some cities still allowed adults to have unregistered devices, but the government had long since made it mandatory for students.

She shrugged. "I keep it offline."

"But why?" Not that I wasn't in favor of sticking it to the government, but the punishment for possessing an unregistered device on school grounds was suspension. That was a hefty price tag to pay for an offline device.

She scrolled nervously. "I just don't like them knowing what I'm reading all the time."

Reading?

I slapped my hand on the table. "It's you."

She flinched and cast a glance around the cafeteria, but as usual the cool kids had given us a wide berth. I dropped my voice and leaned in. "You're the one who keeps uploading Bibles to the school's cloud." The Bible had been banned from the school library because it wasn't inclusive, but someone kept uploading copies to the database. It was driving the principal insane.

"Me and a couple friends, yeah." Abigail searched my eyes for a reaction.

"Rebel," I smirked. Maybe I wasn't the only one in school with a marked file.

I gave her my number verbally. She smiled shyly as she typed it in. "And what's the last name, Thomas...?"

"Smyrna," I answered. "Thomas Smyrna."

AVAILABLE NOW!

WANT EXCLUSIVE BONUS SCENES?

Become a Patron and get access to **exclusive bonus scenes** for this book! This bonus content is not available anywhere else, and I post a new scene every month. Plus, you can get digital ARCs, signed paperbacks, collector's edition hardbacks, and merch, or read my WIP as I write it!

Become a Patron at:
patreon.com/rachelnewhouse

Or sign up for my newsletter and be the first to hear about new releases—plus get sneak peeks of upcoming books, cover art, and more!

Sign up at:
rachelnewhouse.com/subscribe

DID YOU LOVE THIS BOOK?

Please consider leaving a review on Amazon or Goodreads! It's one of the most important things you can do to support an indie author. Thank you!

HI FROM RACHEL

Rachel Newhouse is an author, wife, secretary, and Sunday school teacher from Kansas City, Missouri. Her obsessions are sci-fi, dystopian, and kid lit. When she's not writing, she's cooking Asian food, growing chilis that are too spicy to eat, and watching wildly age-inappropriate shows like *My Little Pony* and *Gravity Falls* with her husband, Joe. She also really likes glitter. You've been warned.

Connect with Rachel:
bio.site/rachelnewhouse